TIME IS A FIRE

TIME IS A FIRE

Vikram Kapur

Srishti Publishers & Distributors
64-A, Adhchini
Sri Aurobindo Marg
New Delhi 110 017
srishtipublishers@forindia.com

First published in 2002 by
Srishti Publishers & Distributors

ISBN 81-87075-79-1
Rs. 250.00

Cover Design by Arrt Creations
45 Nehru Apartment, Kalkaji, New Delhi 110 019
arrt@vsnl.com

Printed and bound in India by
Saurabh Print-O-Pack, Noida

ACKNOWLEDGEMENTS

Several books and magazine articles helped me as I was researching material for this book. Of these the most notable were Shekhar Gupta's articles in *India Today* about Punjab in the early 1990s and Prakash Tandon's book *Punjabi Saga* about the Punjab before partition.

Furthermore, I am indebted to the following individuals for their help and encouragement over the years:

Richard Nordquist, James Smith and Frank Clancy at Armstrong Atlantic State University and Anthony Grooms at the University of Georgia. Without their support in the early days, I would never have become a writer.

Hubert Whitlow of Athens, Georgia, who read and critiqued parts of the manuscript and has remained a good friend over many years.

Doug Cole, a colleague and fellow writer – who patiently read and reread parts of the manuscript and offered valuable advice.

And, above all, my family, my father Brigadier H.L. Kapur, my brother Dr. Vijay Kapur and my sister-in-law Dr. Nandini Sinha Kapur, without whose love, faith and understanding nothing would have been possible.

Contents

THE MONSTER AT REST

The Monster Stirring

CHAPTER
One

In 1984, when Amrita first came to Seattle from Delhi as a sixteen-year-old, she thought there were no days in Seattle; just night and twilight. The sky, when it was not dark, was a steely gray sheet of clouds. Clouds very different from the monsoon clouds she had known in India. They did not bellow or snarl or even so much as grumble. They were simply there. Every so often, as if to remind themselves what they were there for, they released a few drops of rain. Rain very different from monsoon rain. It did not stomp on your roof or plow your garden like shellfire. All it did was flit outside your window, disappearing in a matter of minutes to return you once again to the sky's stoic blankness.

After the incandescent days of India, she felt she had entered a tunnel. With the relish of starving urchins that ransack garbage cans for food, she feasted on the scraps of sunshine, committing each morsel to memory, putting together a store she could savor even on the days she went hungry.

Now, thirteen years later, however, it was the blanket of clouds that comforted her, wrapping her in the security that comes from knowing what to expect from something. And it was the sun that brought shivers of unease, made her feel as she would in the presence of a tease.

She was now twenty-nine. She lived alone in a one-bedroom apartment in Kent – a middle-class suburb south of Seattle. It was, by far, the only home she had known in America. The uncle's house – to which she had emigrated from Delhi after losing her parents – had never been a home. A master's homestead, perhaps, but never a home.

Twenty-nine. Already a spinster. If that fact bothered her, however, she certainly didn't show it. Effortlessly, she continued to sidestep the men her uncle and aunt foisted upon her, the fact that over the past couple of years, the bulk of them had been widowed or divorced not worrying her in the slightest. Her uncle and aunt couldn't figure it out, let alone explain it to a phalanx of disappointed men. "Hi, rubba," her aunt said, with her head in her hands. "What does this girl think she is – a maharani!"

What made matters worse was that Amrita's refusals, far from turning the men away, only spurred them to pursue her that much harder. "Not to worry, Bibiji," they told her aunt. "Tell Amritaji we are wanting no dowry or housework. And if she is not wanting to live with our parents that is okay too; we can live separately."

Still Amrita said no. Needless to say, her aunt found that decision mindboggling. "Is this girl a crack, ji? she asked Amrita's uncle. "No dowry, no housework and what's more – no living with in-laws. And still she says no! And what is wrong with these men, ji? Here is our Harinder all ready to get married, and no man is prepared to talk about it unless we agree to a thousand demands. And there is this girl who shows her boot to men. And what do they do? They queue up to lick it. I am not understanding, ji."

Her husband, however, understood perfectly. He looked at his short pudgy daughter, pouting on the sofa in front of him, and compared her to her cousin – a strapping girl of five-ten with fair skin, long lustrous black hair, large almond eyes and a lovely slim figure to boot – and sighed.

Nowadays, he couldn't think of his niece without feeling more than a little guilty. True, he had taken her in over his wife's objections after the death of her parents. But he certainly hadn't done very much by way of giving her a home. At best he had been indifferent; well, extremely indifferent, not even intervening when he knew his wife was ordering her about like a servant. True, one could argue most men would have acted no differently, considering domestic peace was at stake. But still ... And then he hadn't done too much by way of educating her or improving her prospects in life either. True, he had been hardpressed, raising two children of his own. But ...

Nowadays, his late brother's pictures made him uneasy. Pritam's eyes had an accusing look he found difficult to counter. Who knew in a few years they might be face to face. After all, he wasn't getting any younger. In the meanwhile, he dearly wanted to settle his niece. That would give him at least one saving grace.

Which was why he often took it upon himself to persuade Amrita to marry. Sensing arm-twisting would not work – his wife had tried that long enough – he employed more subtle means. He implored her to think of her parents. If they were alive, wouldn't they have wanted to see her settled? Why, even now, they had to be looking down anxiously from heaven. Then he himself wasn't getting any younger. Who knew when Waheguru might choose to take him? Before that, wouldn't Amrita give him the satisfaction of seeing her settled? Then, at least, he could go to his heavenly abode not worrying what would become of her once he was gone.

Amrita heard him out. Once he was finished, she told him she had absolutely nothing against marriage. Rather, she was all for it. Now if only she could find the right man. Surely in his haste to marry her off, he didn't want her stuck with the wrong man. That wouldn't be what her parents would have wanted either. Right?

He was forced to retreat, saying no; he certainly didn't want that.

Such a tack was typical of her. Early on in America she had learned to use guile rather than frank conflict to get her way. When she was sixteen and barely a month in Seattle, she had protested against being tied to the kitchen all day. Was she some servant hired to cook and wash the dishes? she had demanded from her aunt. Her aunt had simply looked her straight in the eye and told her she should count herself lucky she had a roof over her head and three square meals a day. They were not rich people. Taking her in was really pinching their pennies. Their own children were foregoing things for her sake ... And she, instead of being grateful, was carping over a little housework!

Amrita did not complain again, accepting whatever was assigned to her with a quiet, Yes, Auntyji. She realized resistance would merely worsen the situation. After a while, she figured out most of what she had to do was conjured by her aunt to assure herself that she was squeezing the maximum out of the unwanted orphan in her house. Her aunt didn't really care how well many of the chores were completed or, in some cases, whether they were completed at all. What she did not want was to see Amrita sitting idle.

Amrita made sure she never gave the appearance of being so. With the result, what she actually had to do decreased significantly. However, she also realized she was still very much on her own, as she had been on the night she came home to find her parents murdered.

CHAPTER
Two

She should have been nowhere near her house that night. She should have been on a train – a train bound for Amritsar. Her father had handed her the ticket earlier that evening and dispatched her to the station in a cab – a cab driven by a Hindu driver. He had wanted her mother to go as well. He couldn't very well leave the house all alone and go himself. But he wanted the women out of danger in case trouble erupted in Delhi.

The night of 31st October, 1984. A night where mobs took to the streets of Delhi to teach its Sikhs a lesson; their way of avenging

Indira Gandhi, who had been shot dead by two Sikh bodyguards hours earlier.

Her mother, however, refused to leave. She was staying right there, she announced, with hands on hips and lips set in a firm line.

Her father sighed. He knew better than to argue with his wife. But Amrita had to go, he reiterated. That was no place for children.

Her mother agreed. Yes, Amrita must leave.

So Amrita went. However, on reaching the station, she found herself unable to get out of the taxi. On the way she had seen cars that had been vandalized, shops that had been looted ... She couldn't very well go, leaving her parents in the midst of all that. Why, all the time she'd be sick from worry.

She told the driver to put her bags back in the trunk and turn the taxi around and go home.

When she returned to her neighborhood, however, she found a crowd outside her house. As she alighted from her taxi, she recognized one of her neighbors' servants among the cluster of faces.

"Phool Singh," she called out.

The man came over.

"What's going on?" she asked.

He hesitated. Then he said, "There was a loud noise, Amritaji. It sounded like a gun going off. We all heard it. We came as fast as we could. Your Mummy and Daddy ..."

He swallowed.

"What happened to Mummy and Daddy?" Amrita demanded.

He looked down. Amrita stared at him for an instant. Then she turned and started running towards the house. People stepped hastily out of her way. A voice cried out, "Hey, Ram, it's Amrita." She ran down her driveway to the front door. The front door was open. She burst into the house, shouting, "Mummy, Daddy."

Then she halted abruptly, her voice dying in her throat. There were things scattered all over the floor. The house had been ransacked.

Where were her parents?

"Mummy, Daddy," she screamed. She ran through the hall to the drawing room, trampling over the things strewn in her way. Upon entering the drawing room, she tripped over and fell forward. She started to raise herself back to her feet, then stopped suddenly as she found herself looking down into a pair of eyes; a pair of still, brown, unblinking eyes opened wide as if in surprise.

That was when she realized she was lying on top of her father.

Later, she would learn that her father had been strangled and her mother shot. About the rest of that night, however, she remembered very little. She vaguely recalled being taken to her next-door neighbor Dr. Pant's house, where she was coaxed into drinking a cup of tea. With the tea she was given a tablet which Dr. Pant said would help her. Both the tea and the tablet went down with difficulty. Then Mrs. Pant took her by the hand and led her upstairs to a bedroom, where she made her lie down.

The tablet must have put her to sleep. For the next thing she knew it was morning and she had just woken up. She lay in bed, gazing at the ceiling, wondering why it was green instead of white. Then she realized she was not in her own house.

That was when it hit her. Her parents were dead. Dead. Now her father would never walk into her room to wake her up with a good morning kiss or her mother bring her a morning glass of milk. Now there was no one who'd wait for her after school or wait up for her, despite the fact they had an early morning, on the nights she went out with friends. Now there was no one to argue with on the propriety of going out on a date; no one to share a family dinner or movie or conversation ... Her parents were dead. Once they were cremated, they wouldn't even be flesh and blood. They would exist merely in memory. To see them she would have to look at a picture. Like characters out of a book, they were now people you could merely look at and converse about, but never touch and converse with.

She covered her face with her hands, her back and shoulders jerking, as tears started to flow.

The police still hadn't arrived by that afternoon, although Dr. Pant had called them several times since last night. However, he had managed to get the bodies moved to the hospital morgue. Even that had proved difficult. The riots had brought the entire city to a standstill. There was virtually no traffic. Everyone was staying home and the people working in hospitals were no exception. As a result, the hospitals were grossly understaffed and, therefore, ill-equipped to deal with the emergencies that were being reported from all over the place. However, Dr. Pant, being a medical doctor, had been able to pull some strings.

Late that afternoon, Amrita started asking him about last night.

"Uncle, last night Verma Uncle's servant Phool Singh told me there was a loud noise, like a gun going off."

"Yes, I also heard it. It was round nine, maybe five to nine. When I went outside, I saw that the gate to your house was open. So I went in."

"Were there already people there?"

"No, I was the first one."

"What time did you get there?"

"About nine fifteen I think."

Amrita stared at him.

"It took you twenty minutes to go next door!" she said.

"Amrita, with the way things are in this city ..."

He paused in mid-sentence. Then he looked away. Amrita understood. He had been scared. He hadn't gone outside when he had heard the shot. Instead, he had waited to make sure the coast was clear. And he wasn't alone. Every one of her neighbors had done the same.

What if one or both her parents didn't die instantly? If someone had gone to the house right after the shot rang out, who knew they might have been saved – especially if that someone was a medical doctor.

She rose from her chair.

"Where are you going, Amrita?" he asked.

She didn't answer, just began walking to the front door without once looking back.

She hesitated outside her front door. Then, with a deep breath, she opened the door and went in.

Everything still lay on the floor. There were clothes, books, paper, cartons, boxes ... There were her father's diaries, several volumes of them. For a few minutes she sat next to them on the floor, simply staring at the black binding. Then she reached for a volume and opened it to gaze at the familiar handwriting; the letters, as usual, leaning to the right, the T's never completely crossed, the I's invariably missing the dot on top and everything, as always, in a black fountain pen. The entry on the page in front of her had been made on her fourteenth birthday. Fresh tears filled her eyes at the memory. Abruptly, she shut the volume she had opened.

There were her mother's magazines, her mother's saris and dress catalogues ... And then there were her own things. Her everyday things, as well as things that had been special – things like prizes, good chits, birthday presents ... things like a dog-eared eighth class textbook that, unlike all her other textbooks, she hadn't sold to the junk dealer at the end of the school year. She picked it up and opened it to her favorite reading – the one about Albert Schweitzer and his work in Africa. She remembered the first time she had read it. Upon completing it, she had marched right up to her father and told him she was going to be a doctor.

When she finally put the textbook down, right next to it she found something she had always wanted to forget – a brass plate that she had won as a second prize in a debate. She had stashed it away in the bottom of her almirah. Now she ran her fingers over the cold surface, recalling the heartbreak it had caused. Coming second. She had been sure she would win it all; so sure she had seen herself walking up to the podium and holding the first-place trophy aloft. Yet when the winners were announced ...

And then there were things she found lying about that surprised her. From the floor of her father's study she picked up a *Playboy*, dating back to the sixties. Despite herself, she smiled. It told her that at one time at least, her father had not been as straitlaced as he had always appeared to be.

And then there were other things on the floor that brought new tears to her eyes. In the master bedroom, on the floor right next to her mother's closet, she ran across several letters; yellowing, yet amazingly well-preserved letters. She almost didn't see them. They were partly hidden under a table. And it was with some effort that she managed to retrieve them. They didn't seem to want to come out from under the leg of the table, almost as if they were harem wives, scared her eyes would strip them off whatever modesty they had left.

They were letters her father must have written her mother when they were both young, engaged and impatient to get married. She sat down on the floor and started reading them. As she read, tears filled her eyes. Crying softly, she put them aside. Then she dried her eyes and looked around.

It lay all around her, disassembled, on the floor. A mess of secrets, accomplishments, failures, hopes, promises ... All the pieces that make up the jigsaw puzzle of a life.

She rose to pick them up, as she would shards to dispose in a trash can.

CHAPTER Three

The riots abated only after the army was deployed in Delhi two days after the assassination. By then, the police's role in the riots was common knowledge. In neighborhood after neighborhood, the policewallahs had looked the other way. On countless occasions, they had participated in the killing and looting. It was no wonder that the army had to be called in.

As army vehicles patrolled the streets and jawans did flag marches on major intersections, the rioters disappeared and the people began to dribble out of their homes. They came out cautiously, not staying outside any longer than necessary. After dark, most of the city still resembled a ghost town.

For two days the Delhiites had waited out the riots as they would a natural calamity, clustered inside homes as if in a shelter. For two days they had known the kind of fear that comes in the face of something large and terrifying as a tornado; the kind of fear that reduces people to the status of spectators to the scene of their own destruction.

And now that it was all over, they emerged to find a Delhi very different from the one they had known their entire lives. In several streets, there were bicycles that had been cut up, mobikes smashed to pieces, cars torched black, gurudwaras razed to the ground ... There were also corpses, many of them charred beyond recognition. Others had limbs cut off, faces slashed, heads bashed in ...

A new kind of trash lay about, waiting to be picked up. Not the usual garbage of cigarette and beedi butts, or various kinds of bags, boxes and wrappings made of paper and plastic, or, for that matter, dog and cowshit ... but empty petrol cans whose contents had been used to set people on fire, scorched tires that had been filled with petrol and kerosene and placed as flaming garlands round their victims' necks, and yards of hair. Hair, that was cut after the turban had been ripped off, to be stuffed down its owner's throat.

The Sikhs came out after everyone else. For days many stayed indoors, too scared to venture outside, trying to get by for as long as possible on the food they had stocked up, doing all their shopping through Hindu and Muslim friends and servants. Those who did come out rode to and fro from work in groups, seeking security in numbers, and made sure they were home well before dark.

Several Sikh men had cut their hair during the riots. It was months before they felt safe once again, to let their hair and beard grow and don a turban. Over the next few months, many Sikhs left the city forever. For the most part, they went to Punjab, where their community was in a majority. However, there were those like Amrita, with relatives overseas, who left the country.

CHAPTER
Four

At eighteen Amrita moved out of her uncle's house. She knew if she stayed there much longer, she'd be dumped in a marriage to someone she didn't know and probably wouldn't like if she did. She figured she better leave if she wanted to make something of her life.

However, she didn't simply walk out. She got a job in a McDonald's on the other side of town and pointed out the difficulties in commuting, especially considering she didn't have a car. That way she could keep her relationship with her uncle intact, allowing him to save face rather than be castigated for forcing his orphaned niece out of the house. Whatever else he was, he was the only family she had left.

Over the next eleven years, she saw other girls, instead of going on to college as they'd always said they would, get married and have children. She watched them turn into coarse-faced women with thick waists and a yen for gossip; a replica of their mothers, reliving the life of cooking and early middle-age and husbands that drank too much.

She waited tables, worked in convenience stores and fast-food restaurants ... and went to school. It took five years of working two jobs before she had her high school diploma and enough money set aside for college. And another five to obtain her degree in pre-med. She worked right through college, having already set her sights on medical school.

It was only now, after thirteen years in America, that she finally felt she was getting to where she wanted to be. One more year and she would have enough for medical school. The last thing she needed in her life right then was a marriage.

She was now working as a doctor's assistant. For the most part, she kept to herself. In her free time, she read medical journals. She rarely joined her colleagues when they clustered to discuss their children, their men and women, the whole panorama of their lives ... And when she did, she simply listened, volunteering nothing, responding only in monosyllables ...

Her colleagues wondered about her. They described her as possessed, aloof, one-track minded ... One or two even speculated as to whether she was a lesbian.

Her boss wondered about her even more than her colleagues. She attracted him, had done so ever since she started working for him a year back. Often he was tempted to take her in his arms. But he checked himself. Or, rather, she had checked him. By telling him she had already been promised in marriage to a man in India. A man waiting for his immigrant visa.

He told himself he had a wife and two kids, a successful practice, a position in society ... Yet he wondered: Was there a man in India?

Even people who should have had no problem understanding her did not. There were many like her in Seattle, even more barely a hundred and fifty miles north in Vancouver; Sikh refugees from the aftermath of Mrs. Gandhi's assassination. They formed support groups, associations ... The more militant among them spoke passionately in gurudwaras, participated in demonstrations against visiting Indian dignitaries, joined Khalistan Councils ... She neither joined their organizations, nor attended their meetings. She had turned her back on the past with a finality with which people turn theirs on a war. She didn't reply to the letters that kept coming for over a year after she left India. Even thirteen years later, at the mere mention of the old days, she tuned out or left the room. When Indian governments announced cash awards for those hurt by the 1984 riots and brought lawsuits to bear against alleged miscreants, she refused to pay attention. It was almost as if she had dumped the past in a crate and hammered the nails in. When asked about it, she said she wanted to live not relive.

And there were days where she could almost make herself believe she was over it. Days where she moved through life with the ease of an athlete. Days, where it seemed, she was no different from most people, who had never seen a riot or had their parents brutally murdered ... Not just days, but whole weeks, even months. But even then she couldn't be sure she was truly free, that the past was not biding its time like an infection – a sleeping monster that could start stirring at any moment.

CHAPTER
Five

One November evening in 1997, Amrita found a letter in a white envelope, bearing a Vancouver, British Columbia postmark, in her mailbox. It was evidently in a Punjabi hand. She could guess as much from the Bibi before her name on the outside of the envelope. She was still surprised, however, when she opened the envelope and found the letter written in Gurmukhi. She stood still for a moment, trying to recall the last time she had received a letter in Gurmukhi. Then she wondered if she remembered enough Gurmukhi in order to be able to read it.

Actually, it was less a letter than a note. Nine words in all, scribbled on a white sheet that was so creased it must have been folded and unfolded a number of times, as if the writer, unable to decide whether to mail it or not, kept inserting and removing it from the envelope.

The letter read:

Amritaji, I have to talk to you.

Gurbachan Singh

She put the letter back in its envelope, which she stuck with the rest of her mail in her coat pockets. Then she started making her way to her apartment. She lived at the back of the apartment complex, at the end of a concrete walkway that wound through the middle of the complex in an S. It had rained earlier in the evening. The walkway was muddy and littered with yellowing leaves. Despite her best efforts, stains of mud spread all over her shoes. As she neared her apartment, it began to rain again. She didn't have an umbrella. So she had to hurry.

Finally, she reached her apartment. She kicked off her shoes, put the kettle on for tea, and flopped on the living room couch. Then she switched on the lamp next to the couch and extracted the letter in Gurmukhi from her coat pockets. Again she read:

Amritaji, I have to talk to you.

Gurbachan Singh

She leaned back to sit with her hands clasped behind the back of her head. Gurbachan Singh. She had known a Gurbachan Singh when she first came to America. But he was not from Vancouver; he was a

Seattleite. As far as she knew, he hadn't moved. And even if he had, she very much doubted he'd write a letter in Gurmukhi even if he could; that guy was a cleanshaven Sikh with a haircut who went by the name of Greg!

Furthermore, he'd never call her *ji* – an expression of politeness and respect, generally used when you address elders or people of higher social status. That Gurbachan Singh, from what she could recall, was at least two years older than her, of higher caste, and not too genteel.

No, it had to be the man she had seen at her cousin Harinder's wedding; Harinder, who had finally gotten married little more than a month ago. To a man from Vancouver.

He was an old Sikh, dressed in a white salwar and kameez and a blue turban tied in tiers. He was thin, very thin, with eyes practically buried in their sockets. He had a long beard, extending almost down to his chest, a beard almost completely white. He carried a stick. Yet even with its help, he could barely move. For most of the wedding, he sat by himself in one corner of the hall. When he spoke, it was in a cracked voice. Clearly, it was an effort for him to drag even a few words out of himself. So much of an effort, half were lost in the process.

Who was he? A poor aging relative pulled out of mothballs to keep up appearances on the happy occasion of a marriage in the family? Well, he certainly looked the part. His clothes were wrinkled and faded. And on his feet he wore rubber slippers – crumbling slippers at that.

He was someone she would ordinarily have dismissed with a

pitying glance. Certainly, he wasn't someone she would normally have cared to remember.

As it turned out, however, she couldn't help remembering him. The entire time he was at the wedding, he kept staring at her; staring the way you stare at someone you haven't seen in years and never expected to see again. At first, there was surprise. Then his eyes became quizzical. She could sense him going through a checklist, as he figured out how she'd changed from what he remembered of her. One time she confronted his stare. He dropped his eyes. She wasn't displeased. Even though she couldn't place him, it was apparent he was in some way a part of the life she'd left behind in India; a life she preferred to keep locked away, period.

After he was gone, however, she did ask her aunt about him. Her aunt said he was from the boy's side. Amrita had guessed as much. Her aunt also showed her a card he had presented the newlyweds.

In it he had signed his name – Gurbachan Singh – in Gurmukhi.

CHAPTER
Six

The next day Amrita came home from work to find a note on her front door, asking her to come to the apartment office. When she went over, the girl, behind the desk, took one look at her, and then rose promptly to lock the door to the office even though there was still a half-hour left before closing time. Then she settled in a chair next to Amrita and said, in a voice that was barely more than a whisper, "There were two men asking for you this morning."

She was in her mid-twenties, about five-eight, dressed in black aerobic pants and a white sleeveless top. She had black eyes and straight shoulder-length hair dyed blond. She was new to the apartment complex, the new assistant manager. Amrita remembered reading about her in the newsletter the management put out for residents. She tried recalling her name. What was it? Robyn? Lisa? Crystal? ...

The girl, in the meanwhile, continued to eye her expectantly, obviously waiting for a response to what she had just said. Amrita, however, chose to disappoint, saying nothing. Finally, it was the girl who said, "They wouldn't give me their names. But they did say they knew you. They *were* Indians."

"What did they look like?" Amrita asked.

"Like you."

"I mean were they tall, short ... Did they wear turbans?"

"No, no turbans. The cleanshaven guy I guess was tall – close to six feet I reckon. The guy with the beard, he was shorter."

She leaned forward. Evidently, this was the juicy bit.

"They wanted to know what time you left for work, what time you got back, where you parked your car ... They obviously didn't know you don't have a car. Of course I didn't tell them that. I didn't tell them nothing. I just said we couldn't give out any information about our tenants. The guy with the beard, he got antsy. The other guy, however, took him to one side. I could hear them talking – arguing – in some foreign language. A couple of minutes later the other guy came back and apologized. I could see the guy with the beard wanted trouble. The other guy, however, put one arm round his shoulder and took him away."

The two men had clearly made her day. Amrita could see her perched on the edge of her chair, sharing the experience with her girlfriends in a breathless voice over the phone. Two suspicious-looking foreign men sure beat the hell out of getting bathrooms fixed.

"Thanks for not telling them anything," she said to the girl. "No, I don't think I know them. But I'm pretty sure it's all a mistake. After all, Amrita Gill is a pretty common name among Indians in Seattle."

She didn't bother to explain that was so because a large number of Seattle's Indians were Punjabi. As she prepared to leave, however, she decided to make the girl's week.

"However, for all we know they could be terrorists," she said.

But when she reached her apartment, she settled quietly on her living room couch, without a trace of mirth on her face.

She saw them the next evening. Right after work.

She got off at five. After saying good-bye to her boss, she made herself coffee in a paper cup, planning to drink it on the way to the bus-stop. No sooner than she finished stirring the coffee, however, she paused. That morning had been one of those mornings where the wind had simply refused to let up. It had rammed her the instant she stepped out of her apartment, driving her back into the front door. It was all she could do to hang on to the paper cup in her hand, the cup that is not the coffee in it. No, the coffee leaped out to land on the ground, leaving her contemplating its trickle as also the paper cup crushed in her palm.

So she stayed to finish her coffee, then dug in her handbag for her scarf. By the time she had the scarf on, however, she was late. She ran the two blocks to the bus-stop only to spot her bus in the distance, melting into traffic. Then she realized there was no wind. She tore the scarf off.

That was when she saw him.

He was seated on a high stool by the window in the Starbucks across the street. His elbows rested on the table in front of him, the hands clasped together, the thumbs hooked on a bluish chin. He was clearly an Indian; a North Indian, his fair skin and sharp features suggested. He had short black hair, a long narrow face, black eyes and an aquiline nose made prominent by the hollows in his cheeks. He was dressed in a brown coat, which he wore over a white shirt, and dark trousers. The table in front of him was empty. He was simply sitting, or waiting.

She knew him immediately. She knew those eyes, which stared straight at her, yet saw right through her in their preoccupation with something in the past. She knew those lips pressed together tightly as if to keep from crying out. She knew, even though she was too far to see that, despite its relative youth, it was a well-lined face. So far in America, it was the kind of face she had encountered among cripples doing all they could to drag themselves through one more day. Thirteen years ago in India, however, it was a face that had accosted her constantly – each time she looked in a mirror.

The bus hissed to a stop in front of her, and the intervening years, continents, oceans ... everything that had fallen away slid back in place. Light drops of Seattle rain tapped on her coat like fingertips on a tabla, more urgently with each passing second, causing her to hurry inside the bus.

Once she was seated, however, she sought him out one more time. She had chosen a window seat on the side of the bus that faced the Starbucks. He was no longer alone. And he was on his feet. He was standing with a shorter bulkier Indian man, with a light beard, who was talking excitedly while gesticulating in the direction of her bus.

As she watched, the two men rushed out of the Starbucks. But they were already late. The bus was moving. They were left stranded on the other side of the street. Before they shrank out of sight, however, the bearded man saw her. He said something to his companion, after which he pointed – right at her.

She would never see the bearded man again. His companion, however, she met barely an hour later outside her front door. He stood, shuffling his feet, rubbing his hands together, blowing on them ... doing all he could to keep warm.

"Can I come in?" he asked her.

CHAPTER
Seven

He sat across from her at her dining table. With the exception of the couch, the dining table was really the only place where two people could sit in her living room. She, however, would have felt uncomfortable on the couch, sitting right next to a perfect stranger. The man must have guessed as much, which was probably why he headed straight for the dining table upon entering the apartment.

His presence magnified the room's bareness. All it contained, other than the dining table with the two straight-backed chairs, were a lamp and a couch. And a secondhand couch at that, with coffee stains on the white upholstery. Amrita grimaced. She didn't get too many visitors. It only took one, however, to show how inadequate her apartment was to receive anybody.

The man, however, didn't seem to care. He was busy gulping down a cup of tea, without a thought for the fact it was scalding hot. When he was finished, he leaned back in his chair with a deep sigh.

"Thanks," he said.

She nodded.

He wiped his mouth with a handkerchief. "My name is Deepak Khanna," he said. "I'm from Delhi. I'm a writer – freelance – on the Punjab problem. I came to North America a few days ago to talk to a man. A man I had been searching for the last five years. His name was Gurbachan Singh."

He paused, as if expecting a reaction. Amrita's face, however, betrayed nothing. He continued.

"However, by the time I reached him, he had killed himself."

Now her eyes narrowed. Only slightly, though, and not for long.

"What does any of this have to do with me?" she said.

"Well, Gurbachan Singh was living with his nephew in Vancouver. His nephew owns an Indian restaurant in West End called Mahal. He was Gurbachan Singh's only living relative. He and his wife refused to talk to me. Which was understandable. The entire Punjabi community of Vancouver was up in arms against them. Everyone was saying it was the nephew's wife who drove the old man to kill himself; she wouldn't look after him; she didn't want him in the house; she wanted him disposed off in some old people's home ... In fact, according to some people it wasn't even a suicide; she fed him the cyanide pill that killed him.

"As I wasn't getting anywhere with the family, I decided to look elsewhere. The most logical place was the nearest gurudwara. Where else could a man like Gurbachan Singh turn in the waning years of his life?

"I found many men like Gurbachan Singh at the gurudwara, men that came there practically every day – elderly Sikhs, many of them widowers, who said they had made their peace with the world and were now merely interested in spending whatever time they had left contemplating god. When I sat down and talked to them, however, I didn't get so much a sense of peace as of resignation.

"They were all kinds of men – farmers, government employees, mechanics, truck drivers ... They all came to Canada with visions of spending a comfortable old age only to find sons too busy with their own lives to care about them, daughters-in-law that begrudged them the very roof over their heads, grandchildren who spoke a completely different tongue ... They were lonely men, adrift in a strange foreign country whose language they could not even speak. The only refuge left for them was the gurudwara for no other reason than the fact it was the one place that was familiar; a place where there were scriptures they had learned as children, hymns they had grown up singing, other people like themselves ... They remembered Gurbachan Singh as one of them, as a quiet pious man. In the beginning that was all they were prepared to tell me about him. It took me hours to break down their resistance. Finally, it was one Amarjeet Singh who spoke to me at length about the last few days of Gurbachan Singh's life.

"Gurbachan, he told me, had gone to Seattle to attend a marriage about three weeks before he died. When he came back, he was a disturbed man. He grew quieter than usual. When he prayed, it was clear his mind was not in the prayer. He looked preoccupied, a man wrestling with himself. Amarjeet Singh asked him what was wrong. At first he avoided the question. Finally, two days before he died, he told Amarjeet Singh there was something he had to get off his chest before he could die in peace. He didn't tell him what it was, but he said it was something that happened years ago. He had thought the person concerned was dead, but he had been wrong. He said he was going to write to that person. I asked Amarjeet Singh if he knew who that person was. He didn't. Nobody else at the gurudwara did either. I had no option but to go back to Gurbachan's family. I knew I wasn't going to get anything out of the nephew or the nephew's wife. So I decided to try their children. It cost me a few dollars at the video games parlor. But, finally, I got what I wanted.

"On the last morning of his life Gurbachan Singh gave one of the little boys a letter to post on his way to school. The boy remembered clearly because he wrote the address on the outside of the envelope. You see Gurbachan Singh couldn't do it himself because he didn't know any English. The boy couldn't tell me the whole address. But he remembered it was somewhere in the Seattle area. And he also remembered the name – Amrita Gill."

"I'm not the only Amrita Gill in Seattle."

"Right. But you are the only one whose cousin just married the brother-in-law of Gurbachan Singh's nephew."

"Well, I am sorry I can't help you. I have no letter from Gurbachan Singh. In fact I didn't even know him."

He took a deep breath. "You know I said there was talk as to whether it was really a suicide," he said. "Well, they did find a suicide note in Gurbachan Singh's room; a suicide note written in English."

"But didn't you just say he didn't know any English?"

"Exactly."

He leaned forward.

"You must help me," he said.

"I'm sorry I can't. Like I said I have no letter."

His lips pressed together in a tight line. Then he removed a business card from his wallet and wrote on the back.

"This is my address and phone number in Seattle," he said, handing it to her. "I plan to be here for some time. Give me a call if you change your mind."

He rose. She walked him to the front door. Before opening it, however, she asked, "Who was that other man with you at the Starbucks?"

"Balwant? He was the one who helped me find you. He works for Microsoft. Lives in Bellevue. He is the brother of a journalist friend of mine in Delhi. He knows you."

"He knows me? Then how come I don't know him?"

He looked at her from head to toe. "That doesn't surprise me," he said.

He opened the door, wincing as the cold air hit his face. He paused momentarily, glancing in the direction of the living room couch. Then he buttoned his coat, turned the collars up, thrust his hands in his trouser pockets, and stepped off into the night.

CHAPTER
Eight

She couldn't sleep that night. She tossed and turned in bed, recalling Gurbachan Singh's letter:

Amritaji, I have to talk to you ...

Could the man who wrote that kill himself before speaking with her?

In the morning, she took out Deepak Khanna's card and stared at it for a few minutes. A couple of times, she glanced in the direction of the trash can. When she left for the office, however, the card was still with her in her handbag, right next to the letter in Gurmukhi.

She thought of calling him a few times that morning. The fact she could be the last person, with whom a man who could have been murdered had sought to communicate, made it impossible for her to do her job. Finally, round noon, she took off her white lab coat, picked up her handbag and requested the rest of the day off, saying she had a headache.

Out on the street, she began walking aimlessly. Questions filled her mind. Who was Gurbachan Singh? What did he have to tell her? Could he have been killed because of what he had to say to her? . . . An image of her father floated up in front of her. He was staring at her in his death stare, his eyes still, unblinking and open so wide they appeared to be gaping. She stopped walking, and immediately found herself amidst a cacophony of angry car horns. She was standing in the middle of the road. She held up her hand by way of apology and hurried across to the pavement. There was a Barnes and Noble in the plaza next to the pavement. She decided to go into the adjoining Starbucks for some coffee.

After getting a latte, she entered the bookstore to stroll in the Fiction section, checking out the titles of books stacked in neat rows on the walnut shelves, often pausing to pull one out and check out the blurbs on the jacket.

In her first years in America, she had needed a good story as one needs a blanket on a cold night; needed to wrap herself in the warmth of other lives to stave off the chill of loneliness. With the result, she had devoured books with the appetite of the starving, reading every moment she could steal from her aunt.

That day in the Barnes and Noble, however, the sight of books did not, as it often did, return her to those years. Rather, it tugged her back further, especially when she chanced upon the children's section and found herself staring at books by Enid Blyton and Elinor Brent-Dyer. Books about The Famous Five, The Secret Seven, the school at the chalet ... Suddenly she was back in her house in India, seeking to be done as quickly as possible with dinner and the good night kiss, impatient to climb into bed and, in the light of the bedside lamp, voyage across a whole new ocean of words ...

If there had been a hunger then, it was to explore ...

She turned away, abruptly, stepping away from the entire section, shutting the closet of memories before any could tumble out, once again stalling the past before it overtook her.

Which was when she noticed the man.

He was standing only a few feet away. He was Indian, well over six feet, slim and cleanshaven, with broad shoulders. He was wearing blue jeans and a black leather jacket zipped up to the throat. He had light almost yellow skin, thick black hair combed back from the forehead, and a sharp pointed nose on which a pair of dark sunglasses rested.

When she looked at him, he turned away towards the bookshelves and reached for a book. She stepped past him and made her way to another part of the store. After a few minutes, she stopped and turned around. He was nowhere to be seen. She sighed.

A few minutes later, however, she saw him again. This time he made no pretenses. He simply strode towards her, with hands thrust deep in his jacket's pockets. As he came closer, his right hand emerged. She stepped back. Her eyes darted right and left. She could see nothing except books.

Then, suddenly, he stopped. His right hand dived back inside the pocket. Sensing someone behind her, she swiveled around to see an old white woman in a yellow trenchcoat.

The man stood still, watching her. She stepped back further. As he started to move forward, she swung around and began to run. Her shoes beat like muffled thuds on the green carpet. Her handbag bounced on her thigh. She swerved and wove, bumping elbows, shoulders, knees ... leaving curses in her wake. Through the glass double doors she went, then through the parking lot and across the street, to stop only when she didn't have the breath to go any further.

Panting, she leaned against the display window of a women's store, her face inches from a blonde mannequin in a gray suit. After a moment or so, she turned around. Still breathing hard, she ran her eyes all over to assure herself the man hadn't followed her. Only when she was satisfied did she fiddle in her handbag for Deepak Khanna's card.

The man's hand hadn't stayed outside his pocket for long. Long enough, however, for her to see that it held a knife.

CHAPTER Nine

By the time Amrita called Deepak Khanna, she was composed. Her hands no longer shook. She had wiped her face, combed her hair, touched up her lipstick ... She didn't mention the man with the dark glasses. She simply told Deepak Khanna to meet her in a restaurant within the hour.

If he wanted the letter, he'd damn well tell her what was going on. There was a lot that he hadn't told her the day before. At the time, she didn't want to know. Now she had to.

She arrived almost an hour late, changing buses thrice, going several miles out of her way to make sure no one was following her. She knew Deepak Khanna wasn't going anywhere.

She found him seated at a booth. He was dressed in blue jeans and a red sweater. A thick green jacket lay on the seat beside him, a half-empty cup of coffee on the table in front. When he saw her, he rose. She sat down without so much as acknowledging him. He looked askance, obviously expecting an explanation for her lateness, at the very least an apology.

She said nothing.

Finally, he said, "Can I see the letter?"

"First you tell me what's going on."

"What do you mean?"

"Two days ago I receive a letter from a man I know nothing about. Yesterday you drop out of nowhere and demand to see it. Then today I am followed by a man who wants to kill me and damn near succeeds ... I want to know what the fuck's going on."

He stared at her. She stared back, indignant.

"Okay," he said, finally.

"Do you want some coffee?" he asked her.

She shook her head. He asked the waitress for a refill. Then he leaned back, collecting his thoughts. After a sip of coffee, he began.

"Gurbachan Singh came to Canada in the winter of 1984. Before that he was a peon in the Directorate General of Supplies and Disposals – the DGS and D – in Delhi. He worked there for more than twenty years. What I gathered after talking to people that worked with him, many of whom are still in the DGS and D, was that for a long time he was just another peon. He fetched and carried, took petty bribes in exchange for favors, helped out as part of the domestic help in his boss's house ... He didn't display any unusual interest in politics. Like most people he discussed it only at election time. And what's more – he wasn't even a devout Sikh; he was cleanshaven, with a Hindu wife.

"It was in 1982 that his colleagues began to see a change in Gurbachan. First he grew his hair and beard and donned a turban. Then he started visiting gurudwaras. In the beginning he went only on Sundays. Then he began going practically every day after work. He started getting into arguments, even fistfights, on the question of a Sikh homeland. He began to criticize the constitution for clubbing Hindus and Sikhs together ... In short he became a Khalistani."

1982 was also the year Gurbachan lost his wife. They had never had any children. So he was lonely and miserable. He turned to his elder brother Mohinder, I guess for sympathy more than anything. Mohinder and Gurbachan hadn't spoken in years. Unlike Gurbachan, Mohinder was a devout Sikh who hadn't forgiven his brother for cutting his hair and marrying outside his faith.

"I guess Gurbachan's piety must have begun soon after his rapprochement with Mohinder.

"In 1983, Mohinder and his wife were killed in a scooter accident. Gurbachan took over the responsibilities for his nephew Harkishan – a twenty-year-old boy who worked as a waiter in Gaylord's and dreamed one day of owning his own restaurant.

"It was also in 1983 that Gurbachan started getting close to a Sikh clerk in the DGS and D; a man whose views on the Sikh question were so extreme he was dubbed 'our Bhindranwale' by his colleagues. His name was Kehar Singh."

"Kehar Singh!" Amrita said. "Not the same Kehar Singh who was hanged for Mrs. Gandhi's murder?"

"The very same.

"In the summer of 1984 the gurudwaras were full of men that talked of nothing except killing Mrs. Gandhi. The Bangla Sahib, barely a mile from the DGS and D, where Kehar and Gurbachan spent a lot of their time, was no exception. They were young and old, educated and illiterate, white collar and blue collar ... Men from every walk of life and social class suddenly united by a feeling of humiliation. Just a few weeks back several may have come to blows over Bhindranwale and the whole concept of Khalistan. But then the army had not raided the Golden Temple. The holiest Sikh shrine had not been desecrated ... So where just a few weeks back there would have been argument, there was now near unanimous agreement. The Sikhs had been humiliated. For that humiliation they wanted retribution. And no retribution would be complete until the woman who ordered the army raid had been eliminated.

"On any given day you could have found at least a dozen assassination plots being hatched in the Bangla Sahib. Most of them would never amount to anything, as they were nothing more than a spontaneous reaction to any number of things; a fiery sermon by a granthi, a tale of army atrocities committed inside the shrine, a letter circulated by a senior Sikh government official who had resigned in the wake of the army raid ... More than anything they were a case of angry minds letting off steam.

"As we know now, however, the men Gurbachan Singh was meeting were not interested in merely letting off steam.

"But just who were these men? Was the prime minister's murder merely the handiwork of Beant, Satwant and Kehar; a police sub-inspector, a police constable and a junior-level clerk? Mrs. Gandhi got bullets in her back. How come? Beant and Satwant were crackshots, shooting at her point-blank from a range of less than five yards. Then why were bullet holes found in the roof of her house, which was many yards away? Furthermore, after Beant and Satwant surrendered, why were they shot at? Why was Beant, believed to be the one who planned the whole thing, killed on the spot? Why wasn't he arrested and interrogated? Some claim the shooting was in self-defense. They say Beant and Satwant were shot because they grappled with the commandos of the Indo-Tibetan Border Police. Now tell me, if Beant and Satwant had any intention of getting away, would they have surrendered their weapons? Wouldn't they give themselves more of a chance with a .35 revolver and a Thompson sub-machine carbine than engage in unarmed combat with men specifically trained for that purpose?

"And then there's the whole matter of Gurbachan Singh.

"The last time anybody remembers seeing Gurbachan Singh in Delhi was 30th October, 1984. He went to his office as usual, leaving round five in the evening to go to the Bangla Sahib. Round eight thirty he was seen entering his flat in Karol Bagh.

"After that he and his nephew simply disappeared, dropped off the face of the earth. It took me five years to track them down, that too thanks to a lucky break. A gourmet magazine had done a feature article on Indian restaurants on the West Coast. One of the restaurants mentioned was Mahal, Gurbachan's nephew Harkishan's restaurant. There was a picture of Harkishan. He looked older and no longer wore a turban. He also had a french beard. But I knew it was him the moment I saw the picture.

"According to the article Mahal opened in January of 1985. That means Gurbachan and Harkishan had to be in Vancouver at least by the winter of 1984. Now tell me, from where does a lowly peon like Gurbachan Singh get the money to move his family to Canada and simultaneously bankroll his nephew's dream?"

He sat back. He was finished.

"But where do I fit into all this?" Amrita asked.

"You tell me. You are the one he wrote to."

She opened her handbag and handed him the letter. He snatched it from her hand, dropping the envelope in his haste. After reading it, however, he cursed.

He looked down, the disappointment sitting heavily on his shoulders. Then he raised himself, managing a weak smile.

"I guess this doesn't tell us anything," he said.

He finished his coffee and offered to drive her home. He had a rental car, a white Honda hatchback. They drove in silence. After fifteen minutes or so, they were at her apartment complex.

"What will you do now?" she asked him.

After a short pause, he said, "I guess I will go back to Vancouver and talk to Gurbachan's nephew Harkishan. I am sure he knows something. Possibly he knows a lot. This time I will make him talk."

He turned to her. "I think you should go away for a while," he said. "At least until I get to the bottom of this. It's much too dangerous for you to stay here alone."

Go away. Yes, she could go away. And not just for a while, she could go away forever. She could leave Seattle, as she had Delhi thirteen years ago, and start anew. In the Midwest, perhaps, or even the East Coast. This time she wouldn't be at the mercy of relatives; she had some money saved up. And there were doctors and medical schools everywhere.

It sounded tempting.

However, when she turned to Deepak, she said, "I am coming with you."

She packed a suitcase and accompanied him to his motel, where she insisted on getting her own room. The next day, when the morning was still a gray smear on the sky, they left for Vancouver. Despite the early hour, I-5 was crammed with traffic. It was a while before they could get off the on ramp and slide over into the diamond lane. Amrita sighed when they finally made it. Deepak, seated beside her in the passenger seat, asked, "Is the traffic always so bad this early in the morning?"

Amrita nodded.

He stared at the cars lined up and shook his head.

"It's not as bad as it gets in India," he said. "But here it's all cars. There are no bicycles, no three-wheelers, no manually-pulled carts ..."

"No cows," Amrita said.

He laughed. Near Elliot Bay, however, he looked worried as they encountered fog. The fog seemed to retreat as the car sped forward. To Deepak it appeared to be biding its time, waiting to swoop down and gobble them up.

"Maybe we should park somewhere and wait the fog out," he suggested.

"Relax," Amrita said. "It's only autumn. This is as bad as it gets."

She glanced at him as she said that. Only autumn! Looking at him, you'd think it was the dead of winter. He was dressed in a heavy coat, a muffler, a woolen cap, two pairs of socks, leather gloves ... Surely he missed the sun. The very same hot sun he probably couldn't wait to get away from when he was back home. Well, you only realized how much of a native you were once you became a foreigner.

And what had made him a foreigner? What had made him forsake the sunshine, he had received as a birthright, to shiver in an unheated compact on a murky freeway half a world away? The quest to solve Indira Gandhi's murder? Well, that was what he had said. But why should *he* want to solve it so much? As far as she could tell, he was no detective; he was exactly what he had said he was – a writer. She should know. Her father had been one. Well, at least in his soul.

Why do we do what we do? There is a story in that, her father had told her once, many times a story far more compelling than the one that deals with what we actually do.

Again, she glanced at the man all huddled up next to her. He stared out the window.

CHAPTER
Ten

"How long have you lived here?" he asked her.

They were about thirty minutes outside Seattle. He looked far more at ease now that the fog had dissipated and the sun was starting to edge out from under the clouds.

"Since 1984," she answered.

"Are your parents here as well?"

"My parents are dead."

There was a short pause. Then he said, "They were killed in the riots."

"Yes."

She braced for the inevitable flood of sympathy. By now she had heard it all. He, however, simply said, "Do you want to talk about it?"

She hesitated. She had lived with herself for so long that the idea of sharing herself with someone else was foreign, even scary.

She began slowly, gingerly, as if she were walking on a wet floor. The words dribbled out, interrupted by periods of hesitation. Often her voice faltered. A few times, she blinked back tears. The man listened patiently, letting her go at her own pace, not interjecting anything to prod her along. Progressively, her pauses became fewer and further between, as the words started to flow.

She told him about that night in Delhi, thirteen years ago, when she came home to find her house ransacked and her parents murdered in a riot. Then she told him about her life in her Uncle's house; about moving out and working odd jobs and going to school ... When she was finished, she fell silent, surprised at herself. She couldn't have spoken at such length about herself in the last ten years combined, and that too to a relative stranger. She glanced at him. He hadn't uttered a word during her long monologue, and even now he was silent, his eyes faraway. She wanted to ask where. Her reserve, however, held her back.

Instead, she said, "We are there. Where do you want to go?"

He turned to her. Having been immersed in his own thoughts, he didn't comprehend her question immediately. So it was several seconds before he said, "West End."

When they reached the West End, he told her to park. He said there was someone he had to see, someone he knew in Vancouver who he had asked to check up on Harkishan. He said he'd be back in a few minutes.

As she waited for him to return, the clammy hands of fear ran all over her. She couldn't help thinking that she was standing on the doorstep of a haunted house. A part of her wanted to run. It would be so easy. All she had to do was to switch on the ignition and put her foot down on the accelerator. In less than a minute, she'd be out of there.

She swallowed. She couldn't do that. She couldn't go back and resume her life without getting the answers, not with all those questions clamoring inside her head since yesterday. She forced herself to concentrate on the things around her; the pedestrians on the pavement, the passing traffic, the row of storefronts ... After a while, she felt calmer.

She looked at her watch. Where the hell was Deepak? It had been almost twenty minutes since he left. Who was it he had said he was going to meet? Somebody he'd asked to check up on Gurbachan Singh's nephew?

He'd also said he'd be back in a few minutes.

She decided to give him another five.

However, after only three minutes that seemed like an eternity, she stepped out of the car and fed the parking meter. Then she stood on the pavement, wondering what to do. She hadn't been to Vancouver in years, ever since she moved out of her uncle's house. When she was living with her uncle and aunt, they'd come practically every week. In those days there were few Indian stores in Seattle. So whenever you needed supplies, you went to Vancouver.

However, when she came with her uncle and aunt, they spent most of their time in Surrey, which had a sizable Indian population, not the West End.

She stood there for a few more minutes; a stationary island surrounded by waves of men and women going about their business. She saw all kinds of faces, but not his. She began to walk. A couple of times, she thought she saw him. On closer examination, however, it turned out to be someone else.

She walked to the end of the street. There was still no sign of him. She glanced at her watch. The meter had only a few minutes left to run. She was going to get a ticket if she didn't get back quickly and feed it.

She was halfway there when she spotted him. He was standing in front of a coffeeshop, with a tall man in a long gray coat who had his back to her. She started making her way over to them. Deepak saw her coming and said something to his companion, who turned around.

He was not wearing his dark glasses. But he was the same man who had tried to kill her in Seattle.

The Epicenter

CHAPTER
Eleven

Deepak paced, wondering how to explain everything to Amrita. They were in a motel room. Across the room, the glass sliding doors, which opened up to the balcony, were closed with the curtains drawn. Amrita sat with her back to them, her face impassive, her eyes staring fixedly at the brown carpet.

The door behind Deepak opened. He turned around to see it was Jaswant. He took a deep breath. It was more than a half-hour since Amrita had seen him with Jaswant and turned to run, only to slam into a stocky red-faced man, sprinting to catch a bus, after a few paces. The collision had thrown her on to the pavement, where the concrete had bitten off parts of her knees and forearms. Her handbag had flown open, scattering change, dollar bills, credit cards, hairbrush, lipstick ... all over the pavement.

Deepak had rushed to her, praying she wouldn't scream. To his surprise she did not. Later, he learned it was because she was scared. Not of him but of Jaswant, who had reached her before he did and already had a hand on her shoulder.

More her neck than her shoulder, she would claim later with a laugh. By then she knew Jaswant as he did, as the gentlest of men. That morning in Vancouver, however, she shrank from him. They had to throw her things in her handbag the best they could and hoist her to her feet before marching her off, all bruised and dusty, to the car, holding her between them as if they were two policemen with a suspect.

Now, more than a half-hour later, Deepak finally started to explain.

"Jaswant is no killer," he said. "He is like me – a journalist. We are working together. He never meant to hurt you, merely scare you into showing that letter to me. After I met you the other day we figured that was the only way we'd get to see it. We are sorry for what we did. But you must understand – we have been on this thing for five years. At the time that letter appeared to be everything we had worked for. We simply had to see it."

She continued to sit with her face averted. He turned to Jaswant, who shrugged his shoulders.

That was when she asked him, "Who are you?"

CHAPTER
Twelve

Who was he?

He had been asking himself that question since 1984.

How far back should he begin? From Block 32 of Trilokpuri – on a day where the neighborhood drains carried the sludge of human hair and lifeless arms, rather than washing laid out to dry, dangled from the balconies of houses and Sikh mothers dressed their little boys in girls' clothes and threw their hair open, all in a bid to keep them alive? Or should he go back further? Go back to when he was three and awakened in the middle of the night by people that were sobbing and hugging him simultaneously. He was tired. He wished everyone would go away and let him go back to sleep. He said as much to an especially annoying woman, who was not only wailing at the top of her voice, but also running her long fingernails through his hair, despite the fact he kept jerking his head away. Her hands leaped to her head. "Hi, rubba," she said. "This boy's parents just died and he is thinking of sleep!" At which he turned to his uncle and asked, "What's *died*?"

Or, maybe, he should begin from the day he was born. After all, wasn't that where everybody began?

Maybe there were beginnings he wasn't even aware of. Beginnings that could, perhaps, start to answer the question far better than any one he had in mind. Beginnings that now formed part of a history lost in the madness of partition, as a section of a road washed away by a storm.

He gazed at the woman in front of him, realizing her question had less to do with him than the predicament she was in. She wanted to know him, as one would like to know the epicenter of an earthquake that brings down one's own house.

He settled in the chair facing her and started to speak.

"I will begin in Delhi in 1950," he said. "In Karol Bagh. Yes, Karol Bagh, that merely three years ago in 1947 was a Muslim neighborhood. By 1950, however, all the Muslims had gone, mostly of their own accord, to Pakistan. Those that would not leave had been driven out by Hindu and Sikh refugees from Pakistan. Yes, the dispossessed had dispossessed.

"Karol Bagh was a maze of alleys. Narrow dusty alleys hemmed in on both sides by rows of brick houses jammed shoulder to shoulder. Everything jostled for space. People, traffic, stray animals ... Sometimes it seemed even the sun had to scramble to find a way in.

"Barring a few hours at night, it was a world flooded with noise. In a few years the noise would leap several octaves as motor scooters and motorcycles joined the cacophony, causing old-timers to reflect on the "peace" of the good old days. In 1950, however, the fart of a mobike was still a few years away. All one heard were bicycles jingling their way through the thick human traffic, radios scattering Hindi film songs from the counters of shops and tea-stalls, stray dogs barking, stray cows mooing, hawkers offering juices, vegetables and roasted gram in deep baritones, and conversation ... A ceaseless din of conversation. People talked everywhere. In the alleys, in the shops, and, of course, in the tea-stalls, where they sat on shaky wooden chairs set up next to equally shaky wooden tables and transferred the milky sugary tea from the cup to the saucer to sip with a smacking sound. They talked in Hindi, in Punjabi, in English ... More often than not they talked in all three languages, switching back and forth with the unthinking ease of the multilingual. No, they didn't talk; they shouted. You had to shout to make yourself heard over the din.

"Somewhere in that labyrinth of alleys was an alley that looked no different from any other. An alley where there was, among the usual cluster of brick houses, a house belonging to a schoolteacher named Ramesh Khanna. On a hot summer day in 1950, a ceremony took place in that house; a religious ceremony that made Ramesh's eldest son a Sikh."

"This Ramesh Khanna, was he related to you?" Amrita asked.

"He was my grandfather. I never knew him. He died before I was born. I didn't get to know too much about him either. His sons, my uncle and father, didn't talk about him much. From what I gathered later, I doubt they knew him any better than I did.

"For years he was just a picture, just one more picture in a gallery of lost relatives who wore the marigold garland of the deceased. A portrait, actually, for which he'd posed in a cane chair. In it he wore a red turban, a pair of round glasses, dark trousers and a white Nehru jacket, complete with the rose pinned on the front. He had an in-between face – not round or angular, but somewhere in the middle – a thin moustache, a long slender nose and small eyes behind the glasses. He was smiling. Or, rather, he was trying to smile, and not very successfully at that for he appeared to be grimacing. Obviously he could think of better things to do while sitting in a chair than posing for a portrait. Like reading a book, maybe.

"Yes, I have looked at his picture closely. Not once, but several times since 1984. Before that he could have been a wallflower. After 1984, however, there is nobody I have thought of more.

"Despite my best efforts, he remains an apparition. His name suggests he was a Hindu refugee from west Punjab. But from where in west Punjab? One time my uncle told me Gujrat, another time Rawalpindi, a third time Gujranwalla ...

"To tell you the truth, I don't think Uncle knew, or, for that matter, my father, my father who I knew only slightly better than my grandfather. How come his own sons didn't know? Well, for one my grandfather wouldn't tell them. Moreover, they were much too scared to ask."

"But why?" Amrita asked.

"Well, if there was one way to get on my grandfather's wrong side, it was to ask him about his life before partition. I don't know what it was. Everyone who knew him told me my grandfather was the most mild-mannered man you'd ever meet. He was quiet and patient to a fault, which is not surprising considering he was a schoolteacher . He rarely, if ever, raised his voice and frequently took civility way beyond politeness.

"That is until you started questioning him about his life before partition.

"To this day I wonder why that was the case. Could it be something he did, or did not do? Or was it simply a consequence of what he lost? For, apparently, he did lose a lot. He arrived in Delhi with just the clothes on his back and two little boys that did not have a mother. Other boys, I knew growing up, had a phalanx of aunts, cousins, granduncles ... All I had of my extended family were photographs and, many times, not even that.

"There were times I tried asking my uncle about our family. Not often though, and more out of curiosity than anything else. It was never a long conversation, for Uncle didn't know too much about our family history, frequently not even names of certain relatives. And, anyway, my curiosity was never strong enough to pursue the matter in any detail.

"Did the fact he didn't know too much about his family's history bother my uncle or, for that matter, my father? I think not. The present and the future consumed them far too much. I guess they accepted the lack of a past as someone born blind accepts the lack of sight. I know I did.

"History, however, has a way of catching up with its runaways.

"Who are you, you ask me.

"Well, I think of myself as a splinter, a vivisection, a reed in search of roots ... Maybe all that's part of being Punjabi. Punjab, after all, was first chopped into two in 1947, scattering Punjabis like reeds. Then Indian Punjab was sliced in three parts after independence. And then came the riots of 1984 that once again displaced many Punjabis. Truly, the Punjabi is the eternal refugee.

"How come I am sitting before you today in this motel room in Vancouver? Well, it is the culmination of a sequence of events that began that day in 1950 when my uncle became a Sikh. I can see him sitting there, crosslegged, with a muslin turban on his head. I can see sweat darkening the outside of the turban, sweat flowing in tiny streams down his parchment-colored face as the words flow from the granthi's mouth ... He is fidgeting, and continues to do so despite his father's admonishments. He can't help it. It is a hot summer day, the kind of day where you sweat between your toes. The last thing you'd want on such a day is a turban on your head.

"In fact, that was how my uncle remembered that day. He was only five at the time, much too young to recall dates. Did he have any idea what was going on at that moment? I doubt it. More likely, he wished the granthi would shut up so that he could take that suffocating thing off his head and go play with his friends.

"Would he be alive today if he'd never become a Sikh? Probably. Would I be here today if he'd never become a Sikh? Probably not.

"It is an old Punjabi custom – a Punjabi Hindu family raises its eldest son a Sikh – a relic from pre-partition days, since then largely in disuse. But my grandfather observed it. The same grandfather who did not want anything to do with life before partition. Why? Well, he took that with him to his funeral pyre."

CHAPTER
Thirteen

"I was three when my parents were killed in a fire that burned down a movie theater," Deepak said. "After that I lived with my uncle. A Sikh uncle and a Hindu nephew seems strange nowadays, even farfetched. But then it was neither strange nor farfetched. And we were much more than merely uncle and nephew. I guess I was the child he never had. And he, for all intents and purposes, was my father.

"His name was Sohan Singh Khanna. Few people, if any, called him Sohan or Khanna. The Singh he never even wrote. It was as if he kept his name locked away in a trunk like a family heirloom, bringing it out on the rarest of occasions. Instead, the world knew him as Happy, and he preferred it that way. So much so he named his own business Happy Auto and Truck Works."

"Was he a mechanic?" Amrita asked.

"Yes, he was. You know now that I think about it, he doesn't seem such a big man. In fact, he almost appears diminutive; after all, he was no more than five-seven. When I was growing up, however, I thought he was huge, especially in the early days where I kept trying to scale his trouser leg and falling off.

"I guess some men are meant to be roly-poly, just like some men are meant to be thin as sticks. Uncle, I can't imagine without his paunch. It went perfectly with the round face, the baggy lightly bearded cheeks, the eyes shrunken because of laughing too much ... At least that was what my aunt claimed.

"Yes, Uncle wasn't called Happy without reason.

"Like most modern Sikhs, he curled his beard and sported flashy turbans. He could spend the entire day in a nondescript khaki shirt and pants. But his turban was anything but nondescript. Saffron, red, navy blue ... You name it. Not surprisingly, he considered Namdhari Sikhs, who wear only white turbans, a colorless lot. But then what else, he'd say, could one expect from a bunch of vegetarians!

"Yes, Uncle, like most Punjabis, liked his food non-vegetarian. He once said that if Punjab had to have a state bird let it be tandoori chicken.

"He was very much a man of the world. Practical, fast-talking, constantly scrambling for the next rupee ... More income in a month, a better house to live in ... Such thoughts consumed him. I guess he was as godfearing as the next man. He prayed daily and never missed the Sunday sermon at the gurudwara. However, I doubt very much if his piety sprang from any other need than to observe custom.

"He was often short-tempered with other refugees. He certainly had no time for the ones that sat around all day and talked wistfully of the good old days or the lives they would have had if there were no partition. He often said, 'If there is something wrong with your car you fix it. If it is something that can't be fixed you dump your car and get another one. If you can't afford another car you catch the bus. Whatever you do you keep moving. You never stop. You never ever stop.'

"Did he ever wish he wasn't a refugee? I guess he did. No, he never talked about it. Uncle wasn't a man who shared too much of himself with others. I guess that came with being a refugee and, therefore, an outsider. Very early on, he learned to grin and bear. There were times, however, where the resentment slipped out. One time I remember when he was drunk, he flared up in a rash of epithets against Pakistanis and xenophobic Dehiites that refused to have anything to do with refugees.

"But then, again, I doubt that he could have been the man he was if he wasn't a refugee. You see that was the fuel that drove him in his relentless bid to be a success; that kept him going through all those years of sixteen to seventeen-hour days; that sustained him while he scrounged and saved enough money to show Delhiites that he, an outsider, could come into their midst and build a successful business.

"August 22nd, 1983. That was the day Uncle bought a mechanic's garage in Trilokpuri, across the Jamuna River, and moved us all to a flat near the garage. Even for someone called Happy, that day he was happy.

"Little did he know that a storm was brewing just round the corner."

CHAPTER
Fourteen

"Since the early eighties the newspapers had talked about a group of Sikhs that demanded a separate Sikh homeland," Deepak continued. "By 1984 they had taken refuge inside the Golden Temple and armed themselves to the teeth. For us, however, all that could have been happening on another planet. Not even when Mrs. Gandhi sent the army into the Golden Temple to flush them out were we affected that much. True, some of Uncle's friends were angry. For a day or two I could see that even Uncle was sad. But the moment passed and life went on.

"Until November 1, 1984.

"Some days you never forget. Even years later you continue to live them, almost as if the sun never set. For me that is one such day.

"It looked like any other autumn day in Delhi. The sun was out. Not a pale wintry sun – no, it was too early for that. But not the raging furnace from a few weeks earlier either. No, that day the heat was comforting; a balm rather than a crushing bear hug. There was a breeze blowing as well – a breeze that could have been the fumes of a fire barely a month ago. In the past few weeks, however, it too had changed character. Now it was far cooler and gentler and, consequently, far more welcome.

"To quote my uncle, 'In Delhi you know the summer is over by the end of October, because, by then, your face has had at least a couple of weeks to get used to not feeling as if a dog were panting in it and licking it simultaneously.

"However, if weatherwise it was a typical day for that time of the year, you didn't have to look very far to see it was anything but typical in any other respect.

"For starters, it wasn't a holiday, yet no one had gone to work or, for that matter, gone to school. Usually, when that happened, the men in my neighborhood would drag rope beds out into the alleys, upon which they'd sit and play cards. While waiting their turn, they'd puff on beedis and guzzle sweet tea or country liquor. In other alleys, their sons would play cricket with homemade bats, a tennis ball in lieu of the red leather one, chalk markings on walls in lieu of wickets, and without either pads or gloves. Who had the money for all that equipment? And, furthermore, who really wanted to play cricket? All everybody really wanted was to bat. Bowling and fielding – that was just going through the motions ... However, if a group of girls should happen to pass ... Then it was a whole different ball game, as the bowlers really bent their backs and the fielders dove and slid. And the batters weren't that far behind either. They simply hit the ball harder and farther. Well, they tried to, anyway. Really, it was no surprise that was when a lot of the neighborhood windows got broken.

"But not that day; that day the alleys were deserted.

"In my uncle's flat the aroma of cooking spread from the kitchen. My aunt was making paranthas for lunch. She had made paranthas for breakfast as well. A breakfast that nobody, including her, had touched. I doubted if anyone would touch lunch either. But I guess it helped her just to cook. It was a ritual she performed daily. And in such a situation, you needed a ritual like a cripple needs a crutch.

"Perhaps my uncle expressed a similar need when he said it was high time he went to take a look at his garage. However, he promptly gave up the idea when my aunt and I shrieked no.

"Little did any of us know, however, that, at that very moment, there were men collected just outside the neighborhood. Some of them were actually our neighbors. They were grunting and sweating, as they hauled huge concrete pipes, pipes they were putting in place to cordon off the entire neighborhood. Once they were in place, a few would stay back to man those makeshift barricades and ensure nobody got in or out. The main body, however, would fan out all over the neighborhood. Once they were in place, they would burn, loot, pillage, rape ...

"How could they do that? you might ask. What about the police? Well, the police, as the assailants well knew, would do nothing to stop them. For the police were in on it too, complete with a share of the loot.

"Contrary to most nightmares, this one came in the bright light of the afternoon. Even before we saw it, we heard it coming. There were voices, chanting in unison, Death to all Sikhs, Indira Gandhi zindabad ... There were hundreds of them, armed with knives, machetes, lathis, bicycle chains, car tires and, of course, cans of petrol and kerosene. Their most powerful weapon, however, was something that neither cut nor burned. They had *voters' lists.* Yes, voters' lists that allowed them to pinpoint every Sikh home in the neighborhood.

"Soon glass started to break and feet pounded up the stairs. Through the thin walls we heard our neighbors begging for their lives. Women screamed. Things got smashed. An assailant exclaimed, 'Hey, bhagwan, it's a boy!' He had just stripped a little girl to find it was a boy dressed in girls' clothes ... They were in the flat downstairs. They were in the flat across the hall from ours. And then all too soon, they were at our front door. They were beating on it, demanding to be let in. My aunt was screaming. My uncle and I were trying to push the sofa against the front door ... Then, abruptly, the din subsided. They stopped beating on the door. My aunt stopped screaming. My uncle and I paused. For a few seconds we had an eerie, unreal, pindrop silence ... Then, suddenly, there was a crash – a crash that sounded like a brass gong going off – and the front door hung limply on its hinges. Into the flat they poured, swinging clubs, lathis, machetes ... My uncle tried to stop them. But with what – a mechanic's tools!

"A club hit me on the side of the head and I fell down. Blood streaked my hair. I lay face down, numb, nearly unconscious. Far away, a woman was screaming. Was it my aunt? I heard bits and pieces of shouting, 'Take the turban off. There that's it. Hey, bhagwan, he's bald!' Amidst laughter, 'Pull him by the shoulder, the shoulder ...'

"I passed out."

For a few minutes, there had been silence, as Deepak sat still, gazing unseeingly in front of him. Finally, Amrita rose to get a glass of water, which she offered to Deepak. He accepted it, thanking her. She waited until he had finished drinking. Then she said, "We can stop if you don't want to go on right now."

"No," he said. "It's okay. I'm fine."

He put the glass on the table next to him and continued.

"They burned my uncle alive. They dragged him down the stairs out into the alley, where they emptied a petrol can on his clothes and set him on fire. When I found him he was unrecognizable, his body scorched black as coal. His hands, however, were cold, ice-cold. Even then I remember thinking how odd it was – to be burned and cold.

"I found my aunt in the bedroom. Her mouth was open, a cry stuck in her throat. She had been throttled to death.

"She was also naked.

"When I came to I was still in the flat, lying on the floor. Someone, however, had turned me over. With the result, I lay on my back. Somebody had also placed a cushion under my head and pushed the hair back from my forehead and bandaged the bruise to the head with a cheap red handkerchief.

"Who was that person? I still do not know. When I came to, I was alone in the flat, not just the flat but the entire building. Alone, that is, as far as being alive is concerned. For everyone else was dead.

"Unbelievable as it may sound, my savior could only have been one of the assailants. For no one else could have come close to me in all the time I lay unconscious. The Sikhs in the neighborhood were too busy saving themselves if they were not already dead. The others, if they were not part of the killing and looting, were much too frightened to come out of their homes. And the men manning the concrete pipes would have made sure no outsider got into the neighborhood.

"It must have been a man who was in it for revenge rather than the loot. Someone who decided to make sure if I was a Sikh before dragging me downstairs to burn beside my uncle. He pushed the hair back from my forehead and saw no sign of the blemish that comes from years of wearing a turban, and made a decision. Maybe it was a word from one of the neighbors that prompted him to look; a neighbor, who could have been part of the group that attacked us and knew I wasn't a Sikh.

"I don't remember any of them, not as faces, anyway. I remember them as a tempest, as something powerful and terrifying that smashed everything in a few minutes. A few minutes that changed my life."

CHAPTER
Fifteen

"Lost, I hate that word," Deepak said. "After loved ones die, it chases you everywhere. You hear it from mourners, read it in condolence messages ... Everyone is sorry for what you've lost. *Lost.* It makes me want to say, thank you, now if you should happen to find what I've lost, would you be kind enough to turn it into the nearest lost and found bureau?

"Death doesn't simply kill those that die. It kills something too in those that are left alive. For me the biggest casualty was trust. After the death of my uncle and aunt, I found it impossible to trust anything

– god, friends, neighbors ... just about everything I had believed in until that day.

"So I guess it wasn't surprising I ended up in Punjab; a whole state that found it impossible to trust."

"I was going to make my uncle's worst nightmare come true," Deepak continued. "I was going to be a mechanic. The old man would shout if he caught me anywhere near his garage. At times, he'd throw in a slap or two for good measure. Go to school, he would say, go to college, study, become a big man ... I, however, liked nothing better than to tinker with cars, trucks, mobikes ... just about anything on wheels. Unknown to Uncle, I learned the trade working in a garage in another part of town, when I should have been in class.

"After he was killed, however, there was no way I could be a mechanic. It reminded me far too much of him. I sold the garage and flat. For two years I drifted like a feather without cause or direction, pulling whichever way the wind blew.

"I was down to my last thousand rupees when I decided to go to Punjab.

"Like so many transplanted Punjabis, I had never been to Punjab. Forget about reading or writing the language, I couldn't even speak it properly. Furthermore, I was a Hindu, and Hindus were running away from Punjab in greater numbers than anyone else.

"Then why did I go there?

"Was it because of the questions that had been clamoring for answers in my mind ever since the murder of my uncle and aunt?

Questions such as: Who was I? Where did I come from? Why did my grandfather raise my uncle a Sikh? ... Questions that were part of the far bigger question: How did my life turn out the way it did?

"You know ever since birth we are consumed with the how. How to do well at school? How to get into a good college? How to get this girl or that job? How to raise children? ... Of all the hows there are that is the ultimate how; how do all the pieces fit to make life the jigsaw puzzle it becomes?

"Maybe that was what took me to Punjab; it certainly was the logical place to look for answers.

"Or was it merely another gust of wind that picked up the feather?

"You know as I waited for my bus at the bus terminal in Delhi, there were people arriving from all over Punjab. Busloads of them. People packed inside like fruit in a box; people perched on the roof that had to be hot enough to make the skin sizzle; people hanging on for dear life from the windows ... So many people the buses appeared to be sugar cubes swarming with flies.

"They looked at me; a young man, obviously educated and a Hindu to boot, headed for the eye of the very storm from which they were running.

"They must have thought I was mad."

CHAPTER
Sixteen

"How did you become a journalist?" Amrita asked Deepak.

"By the time I reached Punjab I was down to my last few rupees. I had to find a job quick. I arrived in Jalandhar. There was a newspaper there that needed delivery boys. The man doing the hiring took one look at me and asked if I could write. I said yes. He sent me with a note to an assistant editor. This man asked me a few questions; where I came from, my educational background ... Then he had me write a few pages, after which he offered me a job – that of a journalist, reporting from Ferozepur.

"Yes, Ferozepur, on the India-Pakistan border – the militant heartland itself. The last two journalists the newspaper had sent there were found shot dead. Who would want to go work in such a place, unless, of course, he was crazy, or hungry enough to seek employment as a delivery boy despite having an education."

"You met Jaswant in Ferozepur?"

"Yes."

"And what were you?" Amrita asked Jaswant. "Hungry or crazy?"

"Neither," he answered. "I am simply from Ferozepur."

"Jaswant worked for the local newspaper," Deepak said. "He was a reporter. We met about a week after I reached Ferozepur. Jaswant had just returned, via the night train, from Amritsar, after covering a meeting of Akali leaders at the Akal Takht. In the morning, he had dropped his story off at the newspaper and taken the rest of the day off. He planned to spend it with his nephew, a sixteen-year-old schoolboy, who he was supposed to meet at a local restaurant for lunch. Knowing his nephew, he went to the restaurant ready for an interrogation. The boy would surely want to know all about the meeting in Amritsar: Who was there? What had been discussed? To what extent would the Akal Takht support the militancy? ... So Jaswant went, all prepped up to talk.

"Only to find himself doing all the listening. If he had met his nephew a few hours earlier that wouldn't have been the case. For what Jaswant's nephew told him was a secret. A secret he wasn't supposed to share even with his parents, let alone his uncle. The nephew hadn't foreseen any problems in keeping that secret that morning, when he and two other boys had promised each other their mutual silence. It had all seemed so easy then. In the ensuing hours, however, the nephew had done some thinking, and by the afternoon he was feeling queasy. The more he thought about it, the more uncomfortable he felt. Finally, by lunchtime, he was at a point where he simply had to talk to someone.

"Jaswant and he had just finished ordering, when the nephew, after making sure no one was within earshot, leaned forward and told Jaswant that just that morning he and two other boys had taken a captive; a newcomer to the city who said he was a journalist. Journalist! Ha. What did the man take them for? A bunch of country bumpkins that didn't know all undercover policewallahs posed as journalists?

"At that point the nephew's belligerence evaporated, and concern entered his voice. As he explained to Jaswant, the capturing part had gone like a dream. But now he didn't know what to do with the captive. And what was worse – the others were looking to him to come up with something, for he was the leader.

"I was that captive.

"I guess I was lucky that Jaswant's nephew and his friends were just a bunch of overzealous schoolboys. Jaswant was able to scare them into turning me over to him. I guess he was more concerned with keeping his nephew out of trouble than saving my neck. Once he got me out, he advised me to get out of the area fast. If a bunch of schoolboys could make me a captive, then what chance did I have against real militants?

"I, however, stayed put. Two months later, he was glad I did. For I returned the favor by saving his neck.

"In this case, he was the captive. The militants had just killed two men rumored to be police informers in a nearby village. As it turned out, one of the men killed was actually an undercover policeman. Understandably, the police were jumpy. They were picking up any strangers seen in the area for questioning. One of them was Jaswant.

"The police inspector in charge was convinced he had his man. He ordered the rest of the men released and threw Jaswant in the lock-up with a twenty-four-hour guard. He was so sure he had the assassin. And why shouldn't he be? The man had claimed he was a journalist. Wasn't that what all militants claimed they were?

"So when I arrived a couple of hours later, the inspector was quite happy to talk at length about the dangerous killer he had locked up – one who had the cheek to try to hoodwink him by posing as a journalist. A journalist! Ha.

"You might wonder why he didn't lock me up too if he was locking up anyone who claimed to be a journalist. Well, for one, I had the sense to call in advance. Then I took an issue of my newspaper along, with my byline in it, just in case. Jaswant, on the other hand, was so focused on getting the scoop, he neglected taking any precautions whatever.

"Just think how keyed up I was when the inspector agreed to show me his prize catch. The way he built him up: *This man is no ordinary militant. He is educated, intelligent; he has A-category written all over him* ... God, I was seeing all sorts of headlines in my head. I couldn't wait to get to the lockup.

"And whom did I find there?

"Jaswant."

"You can find yourself in the strangest ways," Deepak said.

"I went to Ferozepur – a place I had never been – to become a journalist, something I never dreamed I could ever be. Yet, the first day on the job, I felt I had done it my entire life.

"Yes, the job saved me. It gave me a reason to get out of bed in the morning, a set of rituals to follow throughout the day, a goal to achieve by its end ... After a while, it became so much a part of me that I couldn't imagine life without it. So much so, when I wasn't working I felt incomplete.

"Soon I was a misfit outside Punjab, among people living lives dominated by money, making good marriages, getting better jobs ... I couldn't relate to men for whom nothing mattered more than home loans and car payments, to women that hyperventilated each time they failed to locate a certain necklace or put on a perfume with the wrong whiff, to children for whom guns were toys with which to play police and thieves ... These were people for whom Punjab was a headline, a dinner-table conversation, an opportunity to roll their eyes and sigh with superior shakes of the head ...

"I found myself hating them, everything about them. I couldn't wait to get away, couldn't wait to get back to Punjab.

"Or was it that I really envied them? For hate and envy are not that far apart. Did I envy them their ordinary everyday concerns, the normal life I was unable to resume after the murder of my uncle and aunt? Did I envy them the fact that they could still trust – in a god, in other people, more than anything in a future? Was I scared that if I got too close to them I'd find myself looking at my life through their eyes, and wondering what kind of man could feel in tune with a life where death was so close so constantly? A madman, or a junkie?

"I spent six months in Ferozepur. Several times I came close to death. Frequently, I was in places where shots were fired. Often I got caught in the crossfire. One time bullets buzzed past my nose like a pack of flies. Another time a bomb exploded in a bus in which I was travelling. Five passengers were killed instantly. One of them didn't even have a face left. I was left bloody all over. None of the blood, however, was mine.

"Yet even then, when I left, it wasn't because of the danger. In fact, what I left to do was just as dangerous. No, the decision, believe it or not, was professional.

"Jaswant, it was, who suggested we join forces and freelance. There was no dearth of stories in Punjab, he reasoned, just of people willing to go out and write them. If we went after them together, there was no telling what we could get. Why, between us, we could take on the entire state. We didn't have to restrict ourselves to an outpost like Ferozepur. We didn't have to be flies nailed to a wall.

"I went back home and slept on it. The next morning I thought about it over a cup of chai. I had a day stretching out in front of me; a day no different from most in the last six months, and probably no different from most in the coming six.

"I decided I was going with Jaswant."

CHAPTER
Seventeen

"So that was when you got interested in Mrs. Gandhi's assassination," Amrita said.

"No," Deepak said. "That happened years later. Before that for five years we combed Punjab. We were in Majha, the Doaba delta, Malwa ... We lived out of a suitcase. We slept all over the place; in sugarcane fields, dried marshes, militant hideouts ... We lived on chai and ate in dhabas. You know what a dhaba is?"

Amrita nodded, recalling a collection of gnarled rickety chairs set up next to equally gnarled rickety tables on a dusty patch next to the road. A dhaba can be found on practically every Indian street. They are roadside restaurants, generally frequented by the poor. Among the well to do, they are often the focus of horror stories about stomach ailments. When she was living in India, Amrita didn't know one well-to-do person who didn't have a story to tell about so and so languishing with dysentery or some other stomach problem because they had eaten at a dhaba. That was why, despite herself, she found herself shuddering at their mention.

Deepak, in the meanwhile, continued.

"Sometimes we were caught up in the rain, torrential monsoon rain, other times in dust storms. In red dust storms where the air suddenly looked like blood spreading from an open wound. In yellow dust storms too. The one I remember most clearly, however, is a dust storm that turned the afternoon sky pitch-black, erasing the sun off the face of the sky like an eraser cleans up a blackboard. It was so dark you couldn't see even a few feet in front. And just a few minutes before you had been squinting due to the brightness of the sun!

"But we got our stories. We got stories on militants, on arms being smuggled in from Pakistan, on police and military maneuvers, on how the people were living through it all ... We made *Sunday*, *India Today*, *The Times of India*, the vernacular newspapers

... Then, in 1992, we talked to a man. Or, rather, he talked to us. Since then there has been only one story for us: How was Indira Gandhi killed?"

CHAPTER
Eighteen

"It was the summer of 1992," Deepak continued. "The entire state of Punjab wore a bombed-out look. Instead of traffic, the streets held mounds of rubble. Come night and whole towns became quiet as graveyards. Forget about venturing outdoors, people didn't even turn on the radio or the two-in-one. The militants had decreed most music decadent. And the news ... Well, that had always been a piece of government propaganda.

"After dark, a cough or a sneeze could be an explosion. The streets were that silent. Even the dogs were quiet. For they were dead, most of them at the hands of their own masters. If the militants came at night and your dog barked, they might very well shoot you rather than the dog. So you couldn't afford to take any chances.

"Nobody spoke Hindi or sang the national anthem. You could get shot for that. And none of the women wore jeans. In fact, they didn't wear anything other than the salwar kameez, not even the sari. All that too was the diktat of the militants.

"Where was the police? you might ask. Well, in many places there was none, and where it was present it wasn't much better than the militants. With the result, you lived the life of a chameleon. If a militant knocked on your door, you opened up with a smile and, with folded hands, offered him a meal. If he asked for money, you paid up. If a policeman came by, you did the same. Always you acquiesced.

"Crazy, I agree. But it was the only way to stay alive.

"Acquiescing alone, however, was not enough to keep you alive. You also had to be careful, very careful, about what you said or wrote. An opinion was a very dangerous thing to voice. Every day people, that were guilty of doing nothing else, showed up dead. Who killed them? Was it the police? Or was it the militants?

"Did it really matter?

"Nobody trusted anything or anybody. Not god or friends or relatives or neighbors or, for that matter, ideas, beliefs and causes. Least of all, they trusted tomorrow. Forget about tomorrow, few trusted the next moment. How could they when they had known so many people that had been blown to smithereens?

"Cynicism abounded, accompanied by a morbid sense of humor. This communist worker's description of a rival group's attempt to kill him was typical:

"'*This man (He broke out in childlike laughter) put a bomb in the bucket of milk delivered to my doorstep every morning. Only it blew up in his face. (He doubled over, laughing.) Not even his spare parts were found.'*

"Yet, underneath all the bravado, fear lurked. You could see it in the many padlocks and boundary walls that had sprung up; in the firearms without which nobody slept; in the armed guards that surrounded even the not so rich. More than anything, however, you saw it when people talked about their children. In low, often tearful tones, they lamented the fact few of the young worked any more. There were simply no jobs; all industry had fled. The dropout rate was going through the roof. And why shouldn't it? What was the point of staying in school if at the end there was no prospect of a better life? It was either the militants or the police, either way the gun.

"Those who could sent their children away. To Delhi or Bombay or abroad to Canada or the Gulf. There was this man Jaswant and I met in a bazaar after an explosion. A Sikh with shards of shattered glass on his clothes. An ordinary middle-aged man dressed in a white pajama and kurta and a white turban. He came up to me and said, They tell me you are not from Punjab, sahib. I don't care where you are from. Just take my little boy with you. I don't care if I never see him again. I just want him out of here.

"Why do you want to send him away? I asked him.

"Why does he want to send him away? Jaswant said. Can't you see why? He's a father. He wants his son to live.

"No, sahib, the man said. Not just to live. More than that I don't want him to kill.

"That is the Punjab into which we will go now. In the middle of the night – curfew time. Be sure to put on your rubber-soled shoes. For here you can't afford to make a noise as you steal through the streets. There are lots of itchy trigger-fingers out there. To tell you the truth, it wouldn't be such a bad idea to pack a gun. Just in case."

"Where are we going?" Amrita asked.

"To listen to a man talk about a cat."

"The first rule in the Punjab of 1992 was that there were no rules," Deepak said. "It wasn't so much a war zone as the Wild West. There were no armies squaring off, simply people; people that sometimes acted alone, sometimes in groups. Nobody joined the fighting; they were sucked into it. Some by the call of cause and religion; some by the excesses of the police and the government; some by the opportunity for loot; and still some by the chance for fame ... Yes, that's right, fame. There were plenty of glory seekers. They were, for the most part, teenage boys drawn to a militant's life for the same reasons their counterparts in the Wild West were drawn to a gunfighter's a century ago ... After a while, however, no matter how or why you got into it, nearly everybody, be it the policeman, the militant or the injured bystander, was in it for retribution. For by then, everybody had lost some family, a lot of sanity.

"Death came at you from everywhere, except where you could see it. Rarely, if ever, it came from the front, always the back or the sides. It could be bullets bursting out of the serenity of a sugarcane field, or a bomb placed in a bucket of milk delivered to your doorstep just like every other morning ... Its messengers too could be amazing. A wizened grandfather of three, a five-year-old boy, a housewife ...

"There were no master plans or rules of engagement. There was simply terror and counter-terror. So the militants kidnapped a family member of a policeman and exacted a ransom. The policeman, in question, would be given a list of the family members of the militants involved. If then he chose to extract his own brand of revenge, the authorities would simply turn a blind eye. Not pretty, not civilized, not even legal. But the kidnappings stopped.

"Yes, once the first bullet is fired, it's no longer about laws or causes. It's simply about winning.

"The walls of the police stations were plastered with pictures of wanted militants. Nothing gave a policeman more pleasure than to cross out a picture with a red pen. That meant the militant had been eliminated. The police used various ways to eliminate militants. Many were killed in shootouts. Others were shot after they had surrendered and a fake encounter was recorded for bookkeeping purposes. Just like the militants, the police had a hit list. If you eliminated someone who was an "A-category" militant, you received a lakh of rupees. That is, officially. Unofficially, the purse could be as much as twenty lakhs – yes, two million rupees, all in cash. I guess it's not surprising that Punjab was crawling with bounty hunters.

"The bounty hunter roamed the Punjabi countryside. Mostly, he posed as a militant, sometimes a journalist. His aim was to hunt down his quarry, collect his reward and disappear. Go far away from Punjab and start a rich new life under a new name.

"The bounty hunter had a nickname: cat."

CHAPTER
Nineteen

"There was no grand design as to how we got the information on the murder of Mrs. Gandhi," Deepak said. "There was a source. We met him in a farmhouse outside Chandigarh – in a windowless room, unfurnished except for a table and three chairs, lit only by candlelight.

"The man's name is immaterial. Suffice it to say he was a smuggler – a drug trafficker across the India-Pakistan border. At least that's what the policewallahs thought. They were quite happy to let him conduct business as he wished. After all, he lined their pockets pretty well.

"However, it would have been a far different matter altogether if the police had learned that he also smuggled arms; arms he sold to militants, dacoits and gangsters; arms that were eventually used against them. Hence all the cloak and dagger stuff. The safehouse in the country, the meeting in candlelight ... The man had secrets to keep.

"How did we learn about him? Well, Jaswant had this source in the Ferozepur underworld who would tip him off on the goings-on from time to time. His front was cheap liquor. In actual fact, however, he was an opium dealer, working for the man in question. Lately, he had started dealing in one more piece of merchandise for his boss – the Kalashnikov assault rifle – brand-new Kalashnikovs fresh from the arms bazaar on the Afghanistan border.

"This man was aggrieved. While his boss was pocketing lakhs in the new line of business, he, by comparison, was slaving for pennies. Furthermore, in the last month or so, the kind of merchandise he'd been getting had dropped markedly in cash value. Other newer dealers were cashing in at his expense. He felt betrayed and wanted to get even, but didn't know how to do that. He couldn't go to the police. It was crawling with informers. Furthermore, he wasn't exactly above board himself. So he decided the best course of action was to tip off Jaswant.

"It took us two months to gather all the information. The tip itself was no more than a pointer. The details we had to collect on our own. Finally, however, we had it all; photographs, names of arms suppliers from across the border ... the whole works.

"Then we got a message: the man we were going to expose wanted to meet us. How he got to know about us, I have no idea. We were discreet in our investigation. But then, again, you can only be so discreet in such things. The man who'd tipped us off originally had disappeared, as if he'd dropped off the face of the earth. Who knows, perhaps his boss discovered he had talked to us.

"Which brings up the question: Why did his boss want to meet us? Why didn't he simply make us disappear as well?

"Well, there are a number of answers to that. By then we were well known. Furthermore, we were presswallahs. If we were murdered, the entire press would be all over the police to find the killer. But then, presswallahs *were* frequently caught in the crossfire between the police and the militants. And the man could surely arrange to make our demise look like such a death. But then, what about the evidence we had collected? For all he knew, it could be sitting with someone who had instructions to send it to an editor in case something happened to us. So, rather than killing us, it made far more sense to try and buy us out.

"Why did *we* agree to meet him? Well, we were curious.

"It's been five years. Still I remember the meeting clearly. The three of us seated in darkness. The candleflame wavering on the table between us. The night outside quiet, except for the sounds of the two men that had brought us there. They had met us after curfew in a Chandigarh side street, and led us through more side streets to a jeep parked at the edge of the city, and then driven us through a maze of dirt tracks to that safehouse. They now stood guard outside with assault rifles.

"The meeting began without handshakes or words of greeting. Straight away we got down to business. Right off the bat, the man offered money. When we refused, he offered information.

"Give me what you have on me, he said, and I will give you the full story on Mrs. Gandhi's assassination.

"What's the story on Mrs. Gandhi's assassination? I asked him. The plot was hatched by Beant, Satwant and Kehar. Beant and Satwant shot her. Beant was killed by commandos. Satwant and Kehar were hanged. Everybody knows that. That's not news.

"So you think that's it, he said.

"What else is there? I asked him.

"So you don't think more people were involved, he said.

"Nobody's proved anything so far, I said.

"Well, there's been talk ..., he began.

"Talk is not proof, I said, breaking him off. With those words, I got up and told him that I was leaving. He asked me to wait and motioned for me to sit down. I glanced at Jaswant, who nodded. Obviously, he wanted to hear what the man had to say. So I sat down.

"The man told us about someone who had been in the Delhi police in 1984. This man, he said, had been a close friend of Beant Singh and knew things about the assassination that nobody knew. He said he could get this man to talk to us.

"How do you know this man? I asked him.

"Well, he said, as you know a policeman's salary is not enough for most men to live on. They have to do something on the side to make extra cash. Well, this man used to sell heroin recovered by the police to me.

"Both Jaswant and I knew how that worked. The exchange was generally made after the show; that is, after the plastic bags of heroin had been laid out on a table for the press to get an eyeful and police officers had expounded on how the heroin had been seized and had their pictures taken. Then, on the way to the police godown or at the godown itself, the bags of heroin were turned over to drug traffickers and similar bags – containing chalk, white paste or traces of vegetable dye – were put in their place.

"I glanced at Jaswant who nodded to indicate that he was game.

"When do we get to meet this man? I asked.

"First you must give me everything you have on me, he said.

"Not until we have met him and heard what he has to say, I said. Then we will make up our minds.

"I said that without thinking, right off the cuff. Beside me, I heard Jaswant catch his breath. Then my own mouth went dry. For a moment, I guess we hovered awfully close to death. Then the man took a deep breath and said he'd set up the meeting. I asked when. He said he'd do it within a week. Once he'd set it up, he'd get in touch with us. Then he rose. As far as he was concerned, the meeting was over. I, however, had one more question for him.

"This man you are talking about, I said. What is he doing now? Is he still a policeman?

"No, he answered, he's a cat."

CHAPTER Twenty

"Three days later we heard from him," Deepak continued. "We were at a dhaba, one of the many between Chandigarh and Jalandhar. There was a note slipped into my hands with a glass of chai by a man I had never seen before, a man who did not bother with pleasantries or stay for explanations. The note mentioned a place and a time and an instruction to destroy it once it had been read. We were to go to the Pavilion – the coffee shop of the Maurya Sheraton in Delhi – two days later at six in the evening.

"We reached the Pavilion a few minutes early on the appointed day. With the exception of a few tourists, it was empty. We made our way over the plush green carpet to a table, which was next to one of the large windows that looked out over the swimming pool. After ordering coffee, we settled down to wait.

"When we finished our coffee, it was almost six thirty. Jaswant suggested we clear the check and leave. He didn't think anyone was coming, but I was willing to give it a few more minutes.

"Ten minutes later, I was inclined to agree with him. I asked the waiter for the check. As I was paying, however, a bellboy came looking for me, holding up a black board on which my name was written in white chalk. He said there was someone waiting for me at the reception.

"It was a man in a white chauffeur's uniform who opened the back door of a white Ambassador when he saw me. On the back seat was a sealed envelope with my name on it. Inside the envelope lay a piece of paper with a room number.

"The Ambassador took us to the Taj Mahal hotel, the Taj near Khan Market, which is miles from the Maurya. You might wonder why they simply didn't call us there in the first place. My answer to that is that they were playing safe. After all, the man we were going to meet was a wanted man; he was a bounty hunter. He had to have several militants after him. And any one of them could have got wind of the meeting and followed us. So calling us to the Maurya, yet having the meeting at the Taj made perfect sense. It gave the driver plenty of time to figure out if he was being followed and lose the pursuer before he delivered us to the cat.

"Finally, we were at the Taj. We went straight to the room and knocked. A man let us in. He was a Sikh, even though he was cleanshaven with short hair. He was a tall slim middle-aged man, with leathery skin, a wide flattened nose and deepset black eyes that had creased eyelids. He wore dark trousers, a long-sleeved madras shirt and a pair of Adidas running shoes. When he spoke, it was with a thick Punjabi accent.

"Clearly, he wanted to be done with the whole thing as soon as possible. No sooner than we were seated, he asked us what we wanted to know.

"I asked him how he had known Beant Singh.

"He said he had been in the Delhi police, same as Beant, from 1974 to '84. That didn't tell us much. So I asked if he too had been part of the prime minister's security. He said no. So, again, I asked as to how he had known Beant. He said he just had.

"I guess I was a little restive by then. This man had kept us waiting at the Maurya, then had us transported to the Taj, and now he was being less than forthcoming. My patience was wearing thin. So I snapped at him, asking if he had known Beant because Beant too was in the business of selling heroin seized from drug traffickers.

"That did it. His eyes fell. He pursed his lips. There was a short pause. Then he told us that he had met Beant when he was attached to the police station in Connaught Place, which was less than a mile from the Bangla Sahib, in the middle of June, 1984.

"He said, at the time, he didn't cut his hair or beard. However, he certainly wasn't devout. He never read the *Guru Granth Sahib.*

And even when he went to the gurudwara he never stayed too long, many times not even for langar. Nor, for that matter, did he pay much attention to Bhindranwale or the Khalistan movement. No, he was more interested in things like his daily bread, the new Hema Malini film, the new cassette by Gurdas Mann ... And in that, one could say, he was no different from most city Sikhs.

"But then, he added, that if I had known him in the summer of 1984, I could have been excused for thinking that religion was all that he cared about. For that was one summer where he went to the gurudwara practically every evening after getting off duty. I asked if he went to the Bangla Sahib gurudwara. He nodded.

"There were many like him at the Bangla Sahib that summer of 1984, he said. Sikhs who, until that point, had little to do with religion, some of whom that barely a few weeks ago might have laughed if anyone had told them that they would soon be visiting a gurudwara every day. They were men from every walk of life, men of various politics – Akalis, communists, even a few Congresswallahs.

"They were men whose calm and ordinary lives had been thrown into turmoil after Mrs. Gandhi had ordered the army into the Golden Temple on the fifth of June. For a while it was easy. Everyone could be angry. After all, the Sikhs had been humiliated. Tanks, mortars and an entire division of jawans had violated their most sacred place of worship, reducing much of it to rubble and leaving what was left standing riddled with bullet holes. For some time every Sikh could vent his anger and rail against those responsible and hatch elaborate schemes to make them pay. But what once that anger wore off?

Could they simply return to their lives and pretend nothing had happened? No, they could not. But then, again, what *could* they do? Most of them were not heroes. They were ordinary men struggling to make a living. They had wives, children, responsibilities ... Everyone couldn't simply run away to Punjab and become a militant.

"So they were confused. More than that they were scared; scared for themselves, their families, more than anything their future ... They sought each other out in gurudwaras. In numbers they sought safety and solidarity. But even more than that they sought understanding.

"It was in this backdrop, our man said, that he met Beant Singh.

"He remarked on how strange it was that Beant Singh had gone on to become a martyr for so many militants. He wondered how many of them would have even cared to shake his hand when he was alive. For Beant, like our man, was a Mazhabi Sikh – a scheduled caste. Furthermore, he had a Hindu wife. True, she had converted after marriage. But she had still been born an unbeliever.

"According to our man, Beant was known as a difficult man to get close to. He didn't trust easily. He was quiet. He kept very much to himself. At times he came across as aloof ... Our man, however, had no problems getting close to him. Being a scheduled caste himself, he understood that Beant's reserve came partly from the fact that he was a scheduled caste. It was an armor he wore against the discrimination to which he was subjected by society. Furthermore, Beant and he had other things in common. They were both in the Delhi police, both sub-inspectors, both none-too-religious men suddenly drawn to a place of religion ...

"At first it was just the two of them. Then came Kehar and Gurbachan.

"I was startled at the mention of Gurbachan. I had heard of Kehar. But who was this Gurbachan? I asked him. He said Gurbachan, like Kehar, was in the DGS and D. He was a peon. At first the four of them were thrown together. As the days passed, however, they met more and more frequently. Soon they were meeting daily at the gurudwara after work.

"According to him, Kehar was the most vocal one. He frequently ranted and raved against Mrs. Gandhi, saying she deserved to die for what she had done. Beant was muted. Most of the time he just listened. He never once raised his voice. The most he said was that Bibi had not done a good thing."

"By Bibi he meant Mrs. Gandhi?" Amrita asked.

"Yes.

"I asked him what Gurbachan was like. He said that Gurbachan was even more silent than Beant. In fact, Gurbachan, he said, reminded him of a student taking notes in class; all that was missing was a pen and paper.

"Why do you say that? I asked. He said it was something in Gurbachan's eyes; the intent way in which he watched everybody, almost as if he was swallowing every word they were saying. When it was time to go home, our man often gave Gurbachan a lift on his scooter to the bus-stop. On the way, several times he attempted to make conversation only to get monosyllables in response. Sometimes he even offered to take Gurbachan all the way home. Being a single man, who lived by himself, he could have used the company. Gurbachan, however, always refused.

"After dropping Gurbachan off at the bus-stop, our man killed time at a chai shop across the street, staying an hour, maybe longer, drinking chai, eating bread pakoras, talking to people ... While he was there, he watched Gurbachan catch his bus. Sometimes he caught a bus bound for Kotla Mubarakpur, sometimes South Extension, somctimes Lajpatnagar ...

"Where did Gurbachan live? I asked him. Karol Bagh, he answered. Karol Bagh! I said. Karol Bagh was miles away from all the places he had mentioned. He nodded and said that was what had got him thinking about Gurbachan in the first place. At the police station where he worked, there was talk of police informers inside the Bangla Sahib; talk that made our man extremely uneasy. You see he also had to protect, as he put it, his 'little side business.'

"Finally, one day, he followed Gurbachan. It was the day before the assassination. By then, a fifth man had joined their group at the Bangla Sahib. He was Kehar's nephew Satwant. Like Beant, he was part of Mrs. Gandhi's security detail. Satwant had just come back from Punjab after a month's leave. He was full of stories of what the army had done inside the Golden Temple, of how the Sikhs were being repressed in Punjab, of how angry the people at home were with the government ...

"Our man recalled the moment clearly. The five of them seated crosslegged on the grass in a circle. The rest of them quiet, listening, while Beant spoke. Yes, Beant – the quiet one. Once he got started he wouldn't stop. It was as if the words had been collecting inside him like raindrops in a cloud and now the cloud had finally burst. Not once did he raise his voice. He was as soft-spoken as ever. Yet what he said was ten times more impactful than all of Kehar's ranting. He looked like a man who had made his peace and now knew exactly what he had to do.

"He spoke of all the years he had spent with Mrs.Gandhi; of how, despite constant self-examination, he could not find an explanation as to why she had ordered the army action. He said he was ashamed. He felt like a traitor to his own people for protecting the life of someone like her. A few days ago he had refused the customary Diwali gift of one hundred rupees she gave to everyone in her household. He wanted absolutely nothing from her. All he wanted now was revenge for what she had done to his people. And that he could only achieve by killing her.

"He said that he and Satwant would do it when Mrs.Gandhi returned from her tour of Orissa. Beant would arrange for Satwant, who was detailed in the outer cordon of security personnel, to swap duties with someone in the inner cordon. Then the first opportunity they got, they would shoot the prime minister. He said that as calmly as if he was planning a day of shooting at the practice range. When he finished, there was silence. Then the rest of them started talking at once. They could scarcely believe what they had just heard.

"Gurbachan, however, mumbled an excuse and left.

"The others were much too taken with what Beant had just said to pay any attention to Gurbachan. Our man, however, was concerned. Gurbachan had just said that he had to go and meet his nephew. Only the day before, however, when he had gone to drop Gurbachan at the bus-stop, Gurbachan had told him that his nephew was in Dehra Dun and would not be back until the 31st. And that day it was only the 30th.

"Our man got up and said that he had to go as well. Then he went after Gurbachan. He rode his scooter to Gurbachan's bus-stop, where he saw him getting on to a bus. The bus was already moving by the time he got there. He decided to follow it on his scooter. Given the traffic and the crowd in the bus it was unlikely that Gurbachan would see him.

"That bus was bound for Defence Colony."

"Defence Colony!" Amrita said.

"Yes," Deepak said. "It's in South Delhi. It's ..."

"I know where it is. It's where I used to live."

CHAPTER
Twenty-one

"Where did Gurbachan Singh go in Defence Colony?" Amrita asked Deepak.

"According to our man, he went to the park in the middle of Defence Colony market, where he sat down on a bench. Presently another man joined him. It was getting dark and our man never got close enough to see this man's face or hear their conversation. But he did say that he was a man of medium height who walked with a limp.

"Gurbachan and this other man talked for about fifteen minutes.

Then they rose and walked out on to the pavement. They were still talking. The man with the limp obviously had difficulty walking, for Gurbachan was helping him.

"The two men parted at the edge of the market, in front of a bakery. I can't quite remember the name he told me ..."

"Auto Bakery," Amrita said

"Yes, that's right, Auto Bakery. After that Gurbachan went home."

"What about the man he met?" Amrita asked.

"Like I said, our man never got close enough to get a good look at him. When he left him, he was still standing outside Auto Bakery. And, anyway, he wasn't his prime concern. His prime concern was Gurbachan. Our man was wondering whether he should talk to the others and confront Gurbachan. However, when he got home that night, he found a police inspector and three constables on his doorstep, waiting to arrest him on drug trafficking charges. Less than twenty-four hours later the assassination took place. By then our man had other concerns. He fully expected to be interrogated for his role in the assassination. But he never was. Instead, he was sent to jail for three years on drug trafficking charges and given a dishonorable discharge from the Delhi police. He never found out who the other man was."

"He was my father," Amrita said.

Inspecting the Ashes

CHAPTER
Twenty-two

Her father had met with a man, who had prior knowledge of the fatal attempt on Mrs. Gandhi's life, in front of her very eyes!

In the morning, she had felt as if she was standing on the doorstep of a haunted house. Now it seemed as if the front door had just swung open.

Deepak and Jaswant waited, watching her. They had been quiet ever since she had surprised them by saying the man Gurbachan Singh had met in the Defence Colony market, all those years ago, was her father. Now they were waiting to hear what more she had to say. She could sense the anticipation building in them.

She closed her eyes. 30th October, 1984 had been a school day, which meant she must have been in school until one thirty. The school bus generally took forty minutes to reach her house. So she would have gotten home by two fifteen. Then she would have had lunch and changed out of her school uniform, after which she would have lain down for an hour before starting on her homework. By four, at the latest, she would have been hard at her books.

As it had been a weekday, her father must have gone to his office in the morning. No, wait a minute. Wasn't that the day her father twisted his ankle? Yes, it was. Her father had twisted his ankle that morning in the bathroom; twisted it so badly he could barely walk. So he didn't go in to work. By the afternoon, he was a little better. But he was still having a lot of trouble moving about. So he was upstairs in bed.

It was six or thereabouts when Mother came to her room and told her she was going to the bazaar to buy vegetables. By then she had completed her homework. No sooner than Mother was gone, she ran to the master bedroom, hoping Mother had forgotten to lock her almirah. She had. Quietly, she opened the steel door. As luck would have it, the latest issue of *Stardust* lay right in front of her. She picked it up and went to her room.

Stardust was off limits for her. Her parents considered her much too young for gossip magazines. However, with Mother out of the house and Father temporarily incapacitated ...

Then ...

She opened her eyes. Deepak and Jaswant tensed in expectation.

"At about six thirty that evening I heard a crash," she said. "It came from my father's room. My father had stayed home that day with a twisted ankle.

(That explains the limp, Deepak thought.)

"I ran up to his room and found him out of bed. He had fallen on to the floor. A pair of trousers was laid out on the bed. Evidently, he was getting ready to change and go out.

"Needless to say, I was surprised. True, every evening my father would go out for a walk. Sometimes it was a short walk, other times he could be gone for a couple of hours. But surely he wasn't going out in *his* state.

"I helped him to his feet. He told me he had received a phone call from district headquarters. It was an emergency, something that couldn't wait. He had asked the man to come see him. He was supposed to meet him in the market in thirty minutes.

"I was confused. I didn't remember the phone ringing. Furthermore, I couldn't see why my father didn't tell the man to come to the house. In his condition, it was obvious he was in no shape to go out.

"I urged him to go back to bed. But he was adamant. He was going, no matter what. When I saw he wouldn't budge, I said okay. He could go if he wanted. But I was going with him. He didn't argue too much with that. I guess he realized he needed the help.

"My mother had taken the car to the bazaar. So we had to walk.

The market was a ten-minute walk from our house. That day, however, it took almost a half-hour. My father had to stop and rest several times.

"When we reached the market, my father told me to sit him down on a bench in the small park in the center. He wanted to speak to the man alone. He gave me money to go buy pastries from Auto Bakery. He told me to wait for him there.

"It took me a few minutes to buy the pastries. Then I stood around, waiting. While I waited, I chatted with the ladies behind the counter. I had been going there since I was five. So I knew everybody. When I saw my father on the pavement outside through the glass double doors, I said goodbye and left with my box of pastries.

"My father wasn't alone. He had a man with him; a Sikh with a flowing beard that fell almost down to his chest. The man was dressed all in khaki – khaki turban, khaki shirt, khaki trousers ... Clearly he was working-class, possibly a peon in some government office going by his clothes.

"I said, Daddy.

"The man looked at me. I was standing under the street light in a red salwar kameez. He salaamed my father. Then he folded his hands to me and said namaste. I acknowledged him with a nod. He turned and disappeared into the crowd.

"I saw him again in Seattle. Thirteen years later."

CHAPTER Twenty-three

"Do you have any idea why your father met Gurbachan Singh?" Deepak asked her.

"No."

"Do you know if he'd ever met him before?" Jaswant asked.

"No."

"Did you ever see Gurbachan Singh before that day?" Deepak asked.

"No."

"Given your father's condition at the time, it certainly would have been the logical thing for him to call Gurbachan Singh to the house. All he had to do was to tell him when he called ..."

"But did he call?" Jaswant countered.

"What do you mean? Her father said there was a phone call. You don't think it was really from district headquarters."

"I know what her father said. But she doesn't remember the phone ringing. And our man in Delhi said nothing about Gurbachan calling someone when he followed him that evening. So I am wondering – was there even a phone call?"

"But why should her father lie?"

"I don't know. But if Gurbachan did call, why didn't her father simply call him to the house? Isn't that what you would do if you were in the state her father was in?"

"Yes, but ..."

"Please, please," Amrita said.

They stopped talking and looked at her. She had her hand on her head.

"I am really tired," she said. "And I have this awful pain in my head. I would really like to lie down."

"But Amrita," Jaswant began.

Deepak placed a hand on his shoulder.

"It's okay," he said. "We understand. We'll be right next door if you need us."

They got up and left. She lay down, feeling exhausted. She was tired of all the revelations, the incessant talking and listening ...

everything that had transpired that day. All she wanted was to close her eyes and go to sleep.

A half-hour later, however, she was still awake. Tired of tossing about, she sat up in bed. The blank face of the TV stared back at her from across the room. She picked up the remote control and started flipping channels. She found nothing that she wanted to watch. A few minutes later, she turned the TV off.

She swung her legs down from the bed and walked out on to the balcony. It was a clear evening. The breeze, however, was more cold than pleasant. Winter was closer than she'd thought in the morning. She stepped back inside.

Half a world away in Delhi, winter would be closing in as well. Or, rather, it would be lurking like an assailant waiting to pounce. For winter did not *come* to Delhi. It grabbed it. One morning it simply pressed its foggy face upon your window, having turned the sun into a fugitive forced to spend long hours in hiding.

That was how Pritam had once described its advent to her. Pritam. For years she had compelled herself not to think of him. But tonight ...

He wasn't a big man. In fact, for a Sikh, he was rather short at five-eight. She certainly hadn't gotten her inches from him. No, they came from her mother – her mother, who was at least two inches taller than her father.

That fact, in itself, set her father apart. There couldn't be too many men in India that married women taller than themselves. In fact, Indian parents worried when their daughter sprouted too many inches; that, in itself, could make her a spinster.

Her father was a light-skinned man, slim and cleanshaven, with brown eyes and closely cropped black hair. Like most upper-class Indians, he dressed impeccably. Not once did Amrita see him leave the house in a torn shirt, or rumpled trousers, or soiled shoes ... In his India the way you dressed indicated your upbringing and social position, or the lack thereof.

As a rule, he wasn't a man who talked too much. At times, he was so quiet, it was hard not to think of him as a fixture, as if he had merged with the furniture and pictures in the room. In fact, going by the letters he wrote, he almost seemed more comfortable expressing himself on paper than in actual conversation. That, coupled with his habit of speaking in analogies, made Amrita think that left to himself, he would have become a writer, probably a poet. However, he came from a generation that did their parents' rather than their own, bidding. So he became a police officer, which gave him a secure job and a respectable position in society – two things every Indian family craves for its sons. He would certainly have made his parents very happy.

Yet now that she thought about it, she wondered how much joy his job or its attendant perks afforded him. Unlike other kids at school, who had fathers in the police or the military, she had never been able to associate her father with car chases, or shootouts with bad guys, or some other daredevil deed. The way those other kids talked, you'd think their dads saved the nation as a matter of everyday routine. She however, preferred to dissociate hers from his profession entirely. Police work seemed so ill fitting for the man she knew. Guns looked much too big in his small hands, sticks far too awkward ... She was secretly pleased when he just about discarded his police khakis in the last years of his life and went about in plainclothes. Anything was more becoming than that awful uniform.

By far, her father was most becoming with a book in his hand. In fact, to overcome his reticence, all you had to do was steer the conversation towards books. Then you had no problem getting him to talk. And once he started, he wouldn't shut up.

On Sundays, more often than not, he was on the prowl for a good book in some library. He would've loved America simply for her public libraries. Those rows upon rows of beautifully bound books arranged in shelves, all cross-referenced and indexed. They were so different from the libraries he frequented that had several books missing, several others with pages torn out, and still others with covers in tatters or spines held together with string, gum, or tape.

Pritam loved books with a passion possible only in someone from an unlettered family. As it was, he was the first one in his family who could read, write and speak English fluently.

"So, Daddy, that means you were the first one to git-mit, git-mit," she said to him when he told her. She had just read that was how Punjabi villagers described spoken English in the time her father was growing up. He burst out laughing.

He told her about the boys that he had known growing up. Boys that loved reading so much they put acrid rapeseed oil in their eyes to keep them open at night, or tied a lock of their hair with a string to the ceiling so that the pull would jerk them awake in case they dropped off. For the boys of his generation, books were more than merely a necessity or a pastime. They were something magical; a potion denied their ancestors they were only too eager to partake to the maximum.

He told her too of the Punjab of his boyhood – the Punjab before partition. He often said he'd marry her off the way girls were married off in the old Punjab. He detested the modern-day weddings, conducted in hotels, where everything was completed on an accelerated schedule. Instant weddings, he called them. She'd never be shortchanged in an instant wedding. He'd make sure of that. Why, he'd even send out her wedding cards marked red and sprinkled with saffron, just like they were in the Punjab he grew up.

(As it turned out, however, it was she who sent out cards for him. Cards she tore from one edge, just as he'd told her bereavement cards were in the old Punjab.)

His eyes would brighten when he spoke to her about his hometown – the great city of Lahore – the Paris of the Orient. Other cities he dismissed as ladies-in-waiting to the queen. "You think Bombay is something," he said to her. "Well, let me tell you Bombay is not even one-tenth of what Lahore was before partition. In Lahore we had everything. It was known as the Oxford of India. Why? Because we had the best colleges and universities. Then we had a film industry. We had more millionaires than anywhere in India. We were the center of culture, of fashion ... The most sophisticated people in India lived in Lahore. Going downtown to the Anarkali bazaar in the evening was an event worth remembering. Anarkali. That name itself should tell you something about Lahore. Can you think of another city that would name its heart after a courtesan?"

His voice would drop perceptibly when he talked about leaving his hometown; of that night in August, 1947, when his father informed the whole family they were going in the morning. The killing and looting were getting worse. There was no police to speak of. Even his father's Muslim friends were urging – leave. It simply wasn't safe to be a Hindu or Sikh in Lahore any longer.

"My father told us all to go to our rooms and choose what we wanted to take with us," he said. "We couldn't take everything. So he said we'd burn what we could not take in the back garden that night. He couldn't bring himself to burn the house. But over his dead body he was going to let anybody get his hands on anything else."

"But, Daddy, how *do* you choose?" Amrita asked.

She was thinking of all the stuff that lay simply in her closet.

Her father was quiet. After a long pause, he said, "Yes, how do you choose? You go back to your room and suddenly everything in it looks precious, even things you haven't looked at in years. The last thing you want is to let anything go. You want to hold on, hold on as you would to a limb despite the fact it has gangrene. That's what fitting a life in a suitcase is all about – deciding which part of yourself to lose, over and over again."

As he spoke, his eyes brightened with tears. He attempted to blink them back, but they leaked out nevertheless, to roll down his cheeks.

A little later, he said, "The world I grew up in doesn't exist today. The world we live in today may not exist tomorrow. Since the beginning of time, worlds have risen only to be reduced to ashes. Time is a fire. It burns down everything. History is nothing, but an inspection of its ashes."

More than thirteen years later in Vancouver, she recalled those words and wondered if, with everything he had lost in 1947, he had also lost his faith. For he was anything but religious. It wasn't simply the fact he cut his hair. He never went to the gurudwara, even for the Sunday sabbath. He didn't read the *Guru Granth Sahib*. In fact, he didn't even keep a copy at home. He never gave donations to temples or godmen. Unlike other parents, he didn't seem to care whether she said her prayers or not. And when Mrs. Gandhi sent the army into the Golden Temple, he didn't appear the least bit affected.

Yet, in front of her very eyes, he had met with a man involved in Mrs. Gandhi's assassination.

CHAPTER
Twenty-four

There was a knock on the door. Amrita opened it. An Indian man, dressed in a dark suit, stood in front of her. He was tall, close to six feet, fair-skinned, with short dark hair, black eyes and a light french beard. He smiled and folded his hands and said, "Namaste." She returned the greeting.

"Is Dhillon sahib in?" he asked.

"Yes. You must be Mr. Singh."

"Ji."

"Please come in."

He entered. The smile on his face, however, froze, as he passed the bathroom door and saw Deepak seated at the table near the far window. He paused. The bathroom door swung open behind him. He spun around to see Jaswant blocking his way out.

"Won't you have a seat, Harkishan," Deepak said.

He had told her about it that morning at breakfast. A continental breakfast. At least that was what the motelwallahs called it. In actual fact, it was muffins and coffee.

She almost missed breakfast. In fact, she would have if it hadn't been for housekeeping. As it was, she was woken up by a short Latino maid who knocked, rather enthusiastically, and asked her if she needed service.

If it hadn't been for that, she would have gone right on sleeping. As it was, it was almost dawn before she finally broke free of the web of memories that had ensnared her to keep her up all night. The moment she woke up, however, she realized the escape had been as temporary as a short furlough from combat.

The past is an irrepressible jailer, Pritam had told her once. She opened her eyes to find herself staring into his, his brown eyes opened wide as if in surprise; the way they had looked before she had closed them for the final time.

The red message light on her phone was blinking; it was Deepak, informing her that Jaswant and he would wait for her downstairs in the lobby for breakfast.

She found them seated, at a round white table, in white straight-backed chairs with circular seats that were padded and covered with red upholstery. Except for them, the lobby was deserted. Breakfast was almost over. There were no more muffins left. Jaswant, however, had saved a couple for her. For that she was grateful, as she was hungry.

She got a paper cup of coffee and joined them. While she ate, Deepak told her that Jaswant had gone to Harkishan's restaurant last night. There he had introduced himself as a banker.

"You see Harkishan's restaurant is losing money," Deepak said. "It's been losing money for some time now. So Harkishan is running around desperately trying to get a loan. We thought since he didn't know Jaswant if Jaswant went there, ostensibly for a meal, and posed as a banker Harkishan would be more than willing to talk to him. You see the situation is so bad that Harkishan has been forced to let many of his waiters go and is back to waiting tables himself. If he doesn't get a loan he could very well lose the restaurant."

"The moment I told him I was a banker he said dinner was on the house," Jaswant said. "Then he sat down at the table and started asking me about collateral and interest rates. I told him I didn't have the information with me. But if he could come and meet me at my motel today I'd be happy to share it with him. He jumped at the chance. He's coming to our room today at noon."

"You don't have to be there if you don't want to be," Deepak said to Amrita.

She didn't hesitate for an instant. "I'll be there," she said.

Now, a little more than two hours later, she was seated at the table with Deepak and Harkishan. Deepak sat to her right, while Harkishan sat across the table from Deepak to her left. Harkishan looked nervous, as he drummed the table with his fingers. More than once, he glanced over his shoulder in the direction of the door only to see Jaswant in the way. Finally, he turned around, despairingly.

"What do you want?" he asked.

"We want to know about your uncle," Deepak said.

"I have already told you everything I know. My uncle was old and ill. He couldn't move about very well. So I guess ultimately things became too much for him and he killed himself."

"After writing a suicide note in English?"

"I don't know how he managed that. But there is nothing I can tell you about it. I simply don't ..."

Deepak jumped out of his chair. With quick strides, he stepped round the table and grabbed a handful of Harkishan's collar. Then he bent down to speak into Harkishan's face.

"You listen to me, Harkishan. I'm only going to say this once. I have been on this thing for five years. Five bloody years. I have been shot at, beaten up, sworn at ... I must have banged on the door of every damn bureaucrat, minister, drug pusher, arms trafficker and god knows who else from Delhi to Chandigarh. I have been to a hundred godforsaken places in Punjab and here I am halfway across the world in this bloody place where it rains every day. And you know what? I am sick. Bloody sick. I just want this damn thing to be over. Now I know you know a hell of a lot more than you are telling. So you better start talking. And start talking soon. Because if you don't I promise you won't get out of here alive!"

Harkishan swallowed.

"Okay," he said. "Okay."

Deepak released his collar. Harkishan sat back, massaging his neck, and asked for a glass of water. Deepak went back to his chair. Jaswant handed Harkishan a glass of water. Harkishan downed it in a gulp. Then he took a deep breath.

"In the last years of his life I grew apart from my uncle," he began. "You know how it is once you are a familywallah. You just don't have the same relationship with your elders any more. Strange, isn't it, when you consider it is your elders that push you to get married in the first place.

"But before that, for so many years there was no one closer to me than my uncle. Not even my father. You see with my father it was almost like he was my boss. It was always Harkishan do this, Harkishan do that ... The two of us never really sat down and talked about anything. But with Uncle it was different. We talked all the time, almost as if we were friends rather than uncle and nephew.

"So many times I told Uncle about my wish to own my own restaurant. Uncle always encouraged me. In that too he was different from my father. I would have been scared to say anything about it to my father. You see for my father a restaurant was beneath me. For him the only work suitable for his son was government service or becoming a granthi.

"Yet despite Uncle's encouragement the dream appeared remote in 1984. I was working as a waiter in Gaylord's. I could see myself working as a waiter for the rest of my life. On what I was making it would be decades before I had enough for a dhaba let alone a full-fledged restaurant.

"I was frustrated. I could see my whole life in front of me. A life of living in a boxlike flat, traveling in crowded DTC buses, taking orders ... always taking orders – never once getting the chance to give them. The life of an ant. Just one more ant among millions crushed under the heel of a big city.

"It was at that time that I met a man from Punjab who had come to address the congregation at the gurudwara. His name was Kuljeet Singh. He was supposed to be a granthi on a tour of Delhi's gurudwaras. In actual fact, he was a militant. His real job was not to deliver sermons, but to recruit people in order to establish a militant network in Delhi.

"I guess I was perfect for him. It wasn't long before he had me convinced that my poverty was all part of a calculated strategy designed to keep Sikhs down. Once I was convinced of that, it didn't take very much on his part to persuade me that militancy was the only way to go.

"So I became a militant. Soon I was carrying messages, both verbal and written. All the messages I carried were in code. I guess I was in a sort of trial period. They wanted to be sure they could trust me.

"I never got beyond that trial period. My uncle learned what I was up to and sent me away from Delhi. At the time I didn't know how he got to know. Later on he told me it was through a man who was supposed to be a police officer, but who in reality was with the RAW."

"You mean The Research and Analysis Wing?" Deepak said. "The intelligence?"

"Yes."

"What was this man's name?"

"Pritam Gill."

CHAPTER
Twenty-five

Her father, an intelligence officer!

Deepak's foot came down hard on hers, causing her to wince. She turned to him. He continued to look straight ahead at Harkishan. Then she understood. He didn't want her to betray herself in any way to Harkishan.

So she kept her face expressionless, not giving the slightest inkling that what Harkishan had just said had surprised her. Harkishan, in the meanwhile, continued.

"Pritam Gill offered my uncle a deal," he said. " He said he would protect me from the police. In return Uncle was to give him information about the goings-on in the Bangla Sahib gurudwara. Uncle was hardly in a position to refuse.

"To get me away from the militants Uncle sent me to live with a friend of his in Dehra Dun. Within days I was homesick. I begged Uncle to let me come back. I promised him I wouldn't get involved in any more militant activity. Finally, towards the end of October, Uncle relented. I booked a seat on the bus that left Dehra Dun for Delhi on the morning of October 31st.

"On the night of October 30th, however, I got a call from Uncle. For some reason he wanted me to leave right away. I told him I had a reservation on the morning bus. He, however, was adamant. I was to leave *at once*. It was only later that I figured out why he wanted me to come right away. He knew that there was an attempt planned on Mrs. Gandhi's life. He feared there might be trouble as a result. So he wanted me home as soon as possible.

"I caught the night bus and was in Delhi early next morning. It was just after five in the morning when I reached home. Most people were still sleeping. Uncle, however, was wide awake.

"I was tired after the journey. So I went to bed right away. When I woke up it was one in the afternoon. I went to the kitchen to make a cup of tea. On the way I found Uncle sitting on the sofa. He hadn't gone to his office. And he looked to be in total shock.

"In a strained voice he told me that Indira Gandhi had been shot. When I heard that all thoughts of tea vanished from my mind. It appeared that Sikhs were responsible for the shooting. That meant there was bound to be retaliation against the Sikhs, particularly in the capital.

"We locked all the doors and windows and stayed in the flat for the rest of the day. We had little food. But we were much too scared to go out. We listened to the radio for any news. But there wasn't much. The radio simply confirmed that Mrs. Gandhi had died and two Sikh bodyguards had carried out the assassination. But it gave us no idea of how things were in the capital or in any other part of the country.

"By early evening everything was quiet. The street below that was usually packed with traffic was empty. All the shops had closed down. There wasn't a street vendor to be seen. It was obvious people believed that trouble was imminent and were staying out of sight.

"The hours passed slowly, and the evening became night. The tension started to tell on me. My head felt as if it would split open. Finally, I simply had to go and lie down.

"I had just settled in my bed when the doorbell rang. Instantly, I was up on my feet. My heart was pounding. I feared the worst. Then I heard Uncle's voice telling me everything was okay. It was someone he knew. Relieved, I sank on the bed and closed my eyes.

"I guess I must have fallen asleep. For the next thing I knew was Uncle shaking me awake and telling me to get dressed. He said we were leaving immediately. When I asked him where we were going, he told me to shut up and do exactly as I was told. There was no time for any explanations.

"We left our flat like thieves, sneaking down the stairs in the dark with nothing more than the clothes on our backs. There was a car waiting in a little side street. We got into the back and the car sped away. For a few miles the driver drove without lights. It wasn't until we were well out of Karol Bagh that he turned his lights on.

"We drove for sixteen hours all the way to Raxaul on the Nepal border, stopping only in deserted country roads to pee and fill up gas. We didn't even go to a gas station. The driver had jerrycans full of petrol in the boot that he emptied into the tank and packets of chutney sandwiches that he shared with us. There was virtually no conversation. The driver never spoke to us other than to ask us if we wanted to eat or tell us when he was stopping to refill gas or take a bathroom break. We never even learned his name. Uncle sat on his side of the seat and watched the road ahead through the window. I thought of speaking up a few times. I had questions. But I kept my mouth shut as Uncle had told me.

"Finally, we reached Raxaul, where we crossed the border on foot. That was the only way for us to get out of India. There was no way we could fly out. After the assassination every Sikh was a suspect.

"There was another car waiting for us on the other side of the border. It took us to the airport in Kathmandu. At the airport the driver handed my uncle a manila envelope that included money, papers and two plane tickets all the way to Vancouver.

"It wasn't until we were in Vancouver that Uncle finally explained things, telling me about Pritam Gill and the work he had done for the RAW."

"Did he tell you who came to your flat that night?" Deepak asked.

"No, he did not. And I didn't ask him either. It wasn't a name I was too keen on learning."

"Why Vancouver?"

"Uncle's idea. He chose Vancouver because it was right on the other side of the world. Also, it had a large Sikh population. It seemed a perfect place for him to get lost."

He sighed, as he added, "Apparently it was not so perfect after all."

He pursed his lips. "There is no point denying it any longer," he said. "It's obvious that Uncle was murdered."

"Why didn't you tell that to the police?" Deepak asked him.

"If I had told them that then I would also have to tell them that he was an informer. I am a familywallah. The moment I tell the world my uncle was an informer for the RAW my whole family will go on a hit list. Remember this is Vancouver. There are plenty of militants here."

"He was your *uncle* for god's sake. He brought you to Canada and set you up with a restaurant. And now that he's dead you don't even want to tell the police that he was killed!"

"Are you a familywallah?" He looked around. "Are either one of you familywallahs?"

When nobody answered, he said, "You can't understand. None of you can understand. You have to be a familywallah to understand."

There was a short pause. Then Harkishan said, looking down at the floor, "Please can I go now. I have told you everything I know."

Deepak didn't respond. Harkishan looked at Jaswant, who nodded. Harkishan got up and left.

After he was gone, Jaswant said, "If he's telling the truth then the intelligencewallahs knew Beant and Satwant would make an attempt on Mrs. Gandhi's life one day in advance. Then why didn't they arrest them? Why did the assassination happen?"

CHAPTER
Twenty-six

Jaswant was on his feet.

"Yes, why did the assassination happen?" he said. "They had an advance warning of more than twelve hours. Then why couldn't they prevent it?"

"Do you still have that map that shows parts of Delhi hit by the 1984 riots?" Deepak asked him.

"Yes, but what will that tell us?"

"Will you just get it out?"

With a shake of his head, Jaswant opened his leather briefcase and removed the map and laid it out on the table. It was a black and white map, with red crosses marking the neighborhoods hit by the 1984 riots. Deepak zeroed in on the lower section of the map that represented South Delhi.

"You said your house was in Defence Colony," he said to Amrita.

She nodded.

"Ashram, Palam Gaon," he read off the map. "Yes, some parts of South Delhi were affected. But none of them was anywhere near Defence Colony. Where exactly was your house located? Was it on Ring Road?"

"No. Our house was way inside the neighborhood, about a couple of miles from Ring Road."

"Was it a big house?"

"No, it wasn't much bigger than most, about four hundred square yards."

"What are you getting at?" Jaswant asked Deepak.

"Listen, the riots of 1984 were not spontaneous. They were organized by local chieftains of Mrs. Gandhi's Congress party. Planning played a big role. An army of thugs was collected and armed. Voter registration lists were obtained to make sure only Sikh homes and businesses were targeted. And the neighborhoods that were targeted were also chosen carefully. Right?"

"Right."

"Defence Colony was not one of the neighborhoods targeted. Why? Because influential people lived there – ex-service officers, rich businessmen, doctors, lawyers, senior government officials ... It was hardly the sort of place where you'd send in gangs of thugs to run amok. After all, it is one thing to trash a poor neighborhood where people have little education or access to power. But you would hardly send gangs of thugs into a place that is home to the kind of people that can get you hauled up. Moreover, those riots did not begin until November first. The people responsible needed some time to get organized. Amrita's parents, however, were killed on the night of October thirty-first."

"So what? After Mrs. Gandhi's death was confirmed on the evening of October thirty-first there were attacks on Sikhs and their property."

"True. But all that was largely restricted to North and Central Delhi and the area around the All India Institute of Medical Sciences. Defence Colony is in South Delhi. It is miles from any of those places. Furthermore, what was the name of that retired Sikh Colonel, the one who was all over the newspapers in 1984 for openly criticizing Mrs. Gandhi after Operation Bluestar? The one who called on the UN to recognize Khalistan?"

"Colonel Amrik Singh."

"Yes, didn't he have a house in Defence Colony?"

"He did," Amrita said. "He had a big house on Ring Road itself. Twelve hundred square yards."

"Exactly," Deepak said. "Now let's say there are some men – two, three, four ... the number doesn't matter. Men, that either live in Defence Colony or close to it, that have been whipped into a killing frenzy by the news of Mrs. Gandhi's assassination. They are out for revenge. So how do they go about getting it? Do they attack a big fat house belonging to one of Mrs. Gandhi's most outspoken Sikh critics that sits right on the main road? No, they do not. Instead, they go down the neighborhood's little bylanes, *in the dark*, to seek out a four hundred square yard house that belongs to an obscure Sikh government servant; a man who has no history of any kind of religious or political involvement."

He turned to Amrita. "You told me your father was strangled," he said.

"Yes."

"When do you strangle someone?"

"When you want to kill without making a noise," Jaswant said.

"Does someone whipped into a killing frenzy worry about making noise?"

"What are you saying?" Amrita asked Deepak.

"I am saying the murder of your parents had nothing to do with the riots. Whoever did it only wanted to make it look that way. That's why the house was ransacked to make it look as if some rioters had looted it. Moreover, I think it was only your father the killer was after. Your mother simply happened to be there."

"But why should someone want to kill my father?" Amrita asked.

"Because your father knew that the RAW had known in advance about the fatal attempt on Mrs. Gandhi's life and done nothing about it. He was the one who received the information from Gurbachan Singh that evening. Those evening walks that your father took were not really walks. That was the time he met Gurbachan Singh every day. Their rendezvous was that park in the Defence Colony market. Most likely your father had put aside a block of time for their meeting, probably an hour. Sometimes Gurbachan was there right at the beginning of the hour. Other times he didn't get there until the very end. That was why the duration of those "walks" varied so much."

"But that man in Delhi told us that after leaving the Bangla Sahib, Gurbachan went to places like Lajpatnagar and South Extension," Jaswant said. "It was only on the day he followed him that he went to Defence Colony."

"I thought he said that Gurbachan *caught buses* that went places like Lajpatnagar and South Extension," Amrita said.

"Okay, so he did," Jaswant said. "What's the difference?"

"The fact he caught buses that were going there doesn't mean he actually went there. You know two days ago when I went to meet Deepak after I thought you wanted to kill me in the Barnes and Noble in Seattle I changed buses thrice. I did it just to make sure no one was following me. That's what Gurbachan could have been doing when he caught buses that went to all those other places. Once he was sure he wasn't being followed, he'd probably get off the bus and catch another going to Defence Colony."

"But then why didn't he do that on October 30th as well?" Jaswant asked.

"Because the information he had was far too important," Deepak said. "In his urgency he neglected to take his usual precaution and, instead, came directly to Defence Colony."

He turned to Amrita.

"You said you didn't remember the phone ringing in your house that evening although your father claimed that he'd received an emergency phone call. Well, I'm pretty sure your father was lying. Your father needed an excuse to get out of the house to meet Gurbachan. The only one that would satisfy you, and keep his secret intact, was an emergency at work. With a twisted ankle, he could hardly be expected to go for a walk.

"After getting the information from Gurbachan, your father must have passed it on. However, there was a screw-up somewhere and the assassination, instead of being prevented, took place. After the assassination, whoever was responsible for the screw-up needed to silence the people who could point a finger at him. Who were those people? Gurbachan Singh and your father. He silenced Gurbachan Singh with money and the promise of a new life for him and his nephew."

"And he silenced my father by killing him," Amrita said.

CHAPTER Twenty-seven

She was standing in front of the bathroom mirror.

A few minutes ago, she had returned to her room, telling Deepak and Jaswant that she was tired and wanted to lie down. In actual fact, she had needed to be on her own. The last couple of hours had revealed a side of her father that she couldn't have dreamed existed. She needed some time to herself to get used to it.

People are like icebergs, her father had once said to her. We see very little of them. The critical part stays submerged, out of sight.

At the time she had nodded, without really understanding what he was saying. Now she wondered if he was talking about himself.

She would have to get used to that part of him.

She would also have to get used to the fact that his death had nothing to do with the riots. She wondered if that was what Gurbachan Singh had wanted to tell her.

She turned on the faucet and splashed some water on to her face. Then she stood for several seconds, with a white towel held against her face. Finally, she took a deep breath and rubbed her face dry.

It came to her just as she was replacing the towel on the steel bar. The towel fell from her hands to lie forgotten on the floor. She stood still, with her forehead furrowed, staring into the distance.

Could it be?

With a quick stride, she stepped out of the bathroom. In her room, she didn't pause for an instant. She headed straight out the door to Deepak's room and knocked impatiently. When he opened up, she brushed past him. He was left staring after her. It was several seconds before he closed the door and went to a chair and sat down. Jaswant, who was seated in another chair, looked askance. Deepak shrugged his shoulders.

For a moment or so, they waited in silence, watching Amrita as she paced in front of them. Then Deepak asked, "What's the matter, Amrita?"

She stopped pacing and turned to him. Her mind was a tumult, a cesspool of frenetic thoughts. She needed to settle them down before she could speak. She took a deep breath. Then she went over to a chair and sat down, facing the two of them.

"A little while ago I started thinking of what Gurbachan Singh would have told me if we'd met," she said. "Well, one of the things he would surely have mentioned was the name of the man who gave him the wherewithal to start a new life in Canada in exchange for keeping his mouth shut thirteen years ago. Clearly that man would not have wanted him to tell me that. Why? Because he was the same man who killed my mother and father.

"Now who could be that man? Well, for one he could only be someone who my father trusted completely. My father would not have trusted just any superior with information as important as what he had received from Gurbachan Singh. He would have only given it to someone he had complete faith in.

"That could only be one man – Ajay Ahuja.

"Ajay Ahuja was my father's boss. He was also my father's best friend, practically his brother. I used to call him Ahuja Uncle. He would bring me presents all the time. He used to say that I was like a daughter to him ... So, at first, the very idea that he could have had anything to do with the murder of my parents appeared preposterous. But then, as I kept thinking, things started falling in place.

"I remembered that when my father came back home after meeting Gurbachan Singh on the night of October 30th, 1984, he dispatched one of our servants Tapan with an urgent letter for Ajay Ahuja. He wanted to go himself. But he had a badly twisted ankle. The effort of going to the market to meet Gurbachan Singh had drained him completely. He was having trouble standing up. So he was forced to send one of his old trusted servants in his place. Even after sending Tapan, however, he only relaxed after Tapan called to let him know that he had delivered the letter.

"Now what could have been in that letter except the information that Gurbachan Singh had given to my father?

"Then there's one more thing. Gurbachan Singh was murdered in Vancouver. In 1983, Ajay Ahuja came to Vancouver on study leave to do his Ph.D. at the University of British Columbia. There he got married to a Canadian girl."

Deepak and Jaswant looked at each other. Then Deepak glanced at his watch.

"It will soon be morning in India," he said to Jaswant. "Why don't you give Ramesh a call. He's an early riser. So he should be up by now. He has good sources at the Cabinet Secretariat. So he should be able to tell us about this Ajay Ahuja. I want to know where this guy is right now."

Jaswant nodded and picked up the phone.

"Ramesh works for *The Times of India* in Delhi," Deepak said to Amrita. "He's a good friend of ours. We've done favors for him in the past. Now it's time to call one in."

They listened over the next few minutes, as Jaswant explained what he wanted to his friend in Delhi. Then he hung up, saying he'd call back in two hours.

"Who was this Canadian girl that Ajay Ahuja married?" Deepak asked Amrita.

"Her name was Rose," Amrita said. "I still remember when he brought her to Delhi in 1984 ..."

Rose and Ajay

CHAPTER
Twenty-eight

Some snippets of conversations overheard on the Delhi social scene, circa. 1984 ...

... "So where did Ajay find this Rose, anyway?"

"Toronto, I think."

"Toronto? I heard it was Vancouver?"

"Arre, yaar. Toronto, Vancouver ... what is the difference? She is Canadian, right."

"Still who is she?"

"I heard she was a student. He met her when he was there on

study leave to do his Ph.D."

"What was he doing his Ph.D. in? Courtship?"

"No, seriously, you heard she was a student. I heard she worked in a bar."

"Really?"

"Does anyone know anything about her family?"

"I heard her father was a poet."

"I heard he was a bus driver."

"You people better make up your mind."

"Well, maybe, he was both."

"O, *come on*, yaar. How can bus drivers write poetry? They are not even matric pass."

"Well, in India they are not. But maybe in Canada ..."

"You know what *I* heard?"

"What?"

"I heard she comes from a titled family. Her uncle is a real Sir."

"*Come on.* That is not possible. I have been to England. There a girl from such a family would never marry an Indian. It can't be that different in Canada. Titled family, my foot! She must be a bus driver's daughter who worked as a waitress or a barmaid."

"Shh, here comes Ajay ..."

... "So how did they get married?"

"O, I bet they got married in a church."

"Really, you think she converted him."

"O, I am sure she did. These *phoren* girls are real chalu."

"Yes, she must have flashed that little smile of hers."

"And fluttered those cat's eyes."

"Uh-huh."

"I wonder what they are going to do with the children."

"O, I bet she got him to agree to raise them Christian."

"Yes, with that little smile of hers."

"And those cat's eyes."

"Uh-huh ..."

... "I wonder what he could have seen in her. I mean other than the fact she's white."

"Well, she looks quite nice. She has long legs. She is slim ..."

"That's what I mean. She is flat."

"Well, she is no Marilyn Monroe. But she is certainly not flat."

"Still what is she compared to him? He is tall, still fairly young, well-settled ..."

"Well, you certainly didn't think he was that eligible when I suggested him for your niece a year ago."

"You suggested him for my niece?"

"I certainly did. And you told me you couldn't very well marry your niece to an old fogy of forty who was a widower to boot."

"I said that?"

"You certainly did. By the way your niece is still not married, is she? And isn't she two years older than Rose? If I remember correctly, your niece must be twenty-seven now, right ..."

That year even Mrs. Gandhi's assassination did not beguile a Delhi socialite more. Just *who* was this woman?

For starters, she was a bus driver's daughter; she confirmed as much. But she also had an uncle who was knighted; she confirmed that as well. Now weren't the two mutually exclusive?

Well, in India they certainly would be. And, as if that wasn't enough, she vexed them even further by confirming that her bus driver father was a poet! Furthermore, she told them she'd been a student and a barmaid. In fact, she'd been both at the same time. Now how could she be a student, as well as a barmaid?

Well, according to her it was easy. She had her classes in the morning, while, in the evening, she worked in the bar. For them it couldn't have been more mindboggling. Students didn't work in bars. And barmaids? Barmaids didn't get an education.

A bus driver's daughter, with a knighted uncle, who was a student as well as a barmaid ... A bus driver who was also a poet ... Hey bhagwan, Canada must be a very strange place.

Then there was the whole question of why she married Ajay.

If she were simply a bus driver's daughter, the answer would have been simple; he represented a leap in status. But there was the knighted uncle ...

A couple of people suggested that maybe she was an Indiaphile. After all, if the newspapers and magazines were to be believed, there were a fair number in the West.

Ye-es, but weren't they, for the most part, a bunch of hippies attracted to all the cheap coke and hashish? the others countered. And, anyway, didn't that craze die out with the seventies?

Others, who were a little more religiously inclined, speculated that maybe she was a Christian zealot who had come to live in their midst in order to convert them. After all, everyone knew that Christian missionaries were the most committed. They went to the most decrepit parts of the country. They lived in villages that had neither safe drinking water nor electricity and were cesspits of cholera, dysentery and god only knew what else ... All in a bid to spread their faith. So it really couldn't be too much of a sacrifice for one of them to marry someone in order to convert him and, consequently, get a chance to convert others. Would it?

Ye-es, the others said, albeit a little doubtfully. For Rose appeared anything but devoutly religious. Her first week in India, she had gone about in shorts and tank tops. (She had stopped doing that since; someone, in all probability Ajay, must have apprised her of their impropriety in India.) Then no one could ever remember her mentioning Jesus or the Bible or, for that matter, even wearing a crucifix and attending church.

Finally, the endless speculation became too much for everybody. So, one day, three handpicked society ladies descended on Rose's house, while the rest of the grapevine chewed their fingernails by their telephones. The three ladies took good care to call in the afternoon, at a time when Rose's husband Ajay was at work. For obvious reasons, they wanted to get her alone.

They waited until the tea had been served and the servants dismissed before coming to the point. Finally ...

"So, Rose, in which church did you two get married?"

"We never got married in a church. We were married in a registrar's office."

"You were? Really? But you are going to bring up your children Christian?"

"I don't know. We haven't talked about it."

"But surely you must have discussed it before marriage."

"No, we did not. We didn't have time. You see it all happened very quickly, in a matter of hours."

The three women looked at each other. A matter of hours! From their experience it took at least a week to simply get a decent dress for the bride.

"And it would have been even less than that if we'd been able to get the justice of the peace at that time in the morning," Rose continued. "You see Ajay proposed to me at six in the morning. And we both wanted to get married instantly. I guess we were scared that if we waited too long we might change our minds. But we had to wait until eight. There wasn't even time to get a wedding dress. I got married in my jeans."

She finished with a smile. There was a long pause, as the three ladies digested what they had just heard. Then one of them asked, "What made you two decide to get married?"

"Well, we were in love."

Now the three women stared at each other. *Love? Wasn't that for the movies?*

CHAPTER
Twenty-nine

Let's go back a couple of years to 1982.

In 1982, Ajay Ahuja was a man with a good job, a position in society and, more than anything, a wife who loved him and whom he loved very much. If there was one thing missing in his life it was children. He and his wife had tried everything from the fertility doctor to the faith healer. To no avail. Finally, they had reconciled themselves to a life without children.

And then his wife became pregnant. Ajay could hardly believe his luck. He fussed over his wife like an ayah. She must not exert herself too much; she must get plenty of rest; she must eat well ... If she so much as sneezed, he was on the phone to the doctor. Every day he counted his blessings. Soon he would have everything he could possibly want out of life. How lucky could a man get.

When the time came, however, rather than getting it all, he lost it all.

A caesarian birth gone awry; the mother dead, the child stillborn ...

Friends and relatives gathered round him. There was a funeral, a cremation. There was a prayer meeting, where the pundit recited couplets from *The Bhagwat Gita*. There was a keertan, where gospel singers sang devotional songs. There was a pilgrimage to the Ganges to immerse the dead ashes ... And then everyone went back home. Within days, they were all sewn back into the fabric of their lives.

Ajay, too, attempted to return to his life, only to find he had no appetite for any part of it – not his job, not his home, not any one of his clubs ... Dark circles crowded round his eyes, as he found it impossible to sleep. His once immaculate appearance rapidly became disheveled. His shirts were rumpled and stained with food. His hair looked decidedly messy, as he fell out of the habit of either running a comb through it or getting it cut regularly. An untidy stubble sprouted on his chin ... He started to miss work – at first occasionally, then frequently – without so much as bothering to call in. When his office attempted to reach him, more often than not, the phone simply kept ringing. On the rare occasions he answered, his speech was invariably slurred.

Friends and relatives endeavored to help. More than a few told him to put the past behind and move on. They implored him to remarry. To help matters along, they dropped names of women that had recently been divorced or widowed. A few even suggested placing a matrimonial ad in the newspaper.

Ajay heard them all out without comment. Inwardly, however, he burned. What did these people think? That a wife could be replaced as easily as a shirt? In one of his weaker moments he spoke candidly to his best friend, Pritam Gill – one of the few people he knew who hadn't yet pitched remarriage. Pritam and Ajay had been best friends for years. They were both Punjabi refugees from West Pakistan. They had first met as colleagues in the Delhi police from where they had been transferred to the RAW. They were both still in the RAW. Ajay, in fact, was Pritam's boss.

Pritam listened to what Ajay had to say. Then he said, "I know what you mean. I would feel the same too if I lost my wife."

"Then why don't *they*?" Ajay demanded. "They all have wives too."

"That doesn't mean they love them," Pritam said. "Love and marriage are not the same thing."

It pained Pritam to see the way his friend was deteriorating. He tried to do the best he could to reverse the trend. He spent as much time as he could with Ajay. Repeatedly, he asked Ajay to come over to his house. Come and have dinner with us, he said. Spend the night. Don't stand on formality. It's just like your own home.

At first, Ajay accepted Pritam's invitation. Soon, however, he started to refuse. Even when Pritam pressed him, he stuck to his guns, invariably coming up with a reason with which Pritam couldn't argue. Sometimes he had a prior commitment; other times he was catching up on work; and, at still other times, he wasn't feeling well ... The real reason he never once hinted at; never let on to the fact that he was loneliest among friends – in their homes – where the presence of wives and children made him that much more aware of the empty house to which he had to eventually return.

As the days passed, Ajay felt more and more caged in. Everywhere he turned, a memory from his former life lay in wait. Staying home was unbearable. Going out wasn't that much better. On every street there were places he had visited with his wife over the years ... More memories. And still more memories.

He had to get away. There could be no peace for him in that city where he and his wife had met and married and lived together for fifteen years. He approached his boss, telling him he wanted to go on study leave to do his Ph.D. His boss didn't ask too many questions. He was an old friend. He understood. He approved the request and wished him the best of luck.

So Ajay left for Vancouver to do his Ph.D. at the University of British Columbia, thinking that now, at last, he was making a new beginning. He had never been to Vancouver, nor did he know anyone from there. It was an entirely new city – just the kind of place where he could finally break free from the stranglehold of the past.

When he arrived in Vancouver, however, he felt far from free; he felt lost.

Soon after landing, he was coughing and sneezing. The cold weather had caught him unawares. Before coming, he had known it could get really cold in Canada. But he had thought that was only in winter. Coming from Delhi, he was used to four distinct seasons. What he didn't know was that it could get cold at any time in Vancouver. Later, he would learn that what was warm for a Vancouver native was cold for him, anyway.

He found his residence to be a dorm room that he shared with a roommate. A ten by twelve-foot room, with walls painted blue – a room that was bare, except for a couple of desks and two squeaky beds. His bathroom was a large communal bathroom used by fifteen other students. To do laundry he had to walk two floors down to the laundry room ... Needless to say, all of that was quite a departure from his life in India, where he had a fully furnished eight hundred square-yard house and servants to do his bidding.

His roommate was a man from China who didn't speak any English. Ajay didn't have a car. He didn't know how to cook. The first few days, he lived on bread and coffee.

On the first morning of the new semester, he walked to his first class, feeling more and more alienated with each step. He was a foreigner, an Eastern man in a Western country, a man pushing forty on a campus swarming with teenagers and twenty-somethings ... He entered his classroom to halt just inside the door and stood, staring at the other students. All those young men and women, dressed in jeans and T-shirts, introducing themselves to each other as if it were the most natural thing in the world. He had to be at least ten years older than the lot of them.

At that moment, a woman came up to him and started talking – a tall slim white woman with long brown hair. A woman who was not a professor or a counselor or anyone else paid to talk to him, as just about everyone who had spoken to him so far in Vancouver had been. He found himself unable to utter a word. He was so completely overwhelmed.

Later, Rose told him he had reminded her of her grandfather, standing there just inside the classroom door. At first, she had thought he was the professor. He was dressed in a suit and a pair of black shoes. His glasses made him look intellectual. The gray in his sideburns gave him an air of distinction. (You mean it made me look older, he said, when she told him. They both laughed at that.) She expected him to stride to the top of the room and call the class to order. She even started taking her books out of her bag.

But he stopped dead just inside the doorway. His eyes became furtive, his brows knitted, he swallowed and started to sweat ... Suddenly he looked scared, trapped, clueless ... In that instant, he reminded her of her grandfather; her grandfather who was Lebanese and could not speak English. One day when she was fourteen, she had taken her grandfather to the shopping arcade. He had arthritis in both knees, which made it difficult for him to walk. So she bought him a coffee and left him sitting in a coffee shop, promising she'd be back in fifteen to twenty minutes, a half-hour max. Once she got into her shopping, however, she lost all track of time. In no time, an hour had passed. She ran back to the coffee shop to find her grandfather still there, sitting exactly where she had left him, but looking panic-stricken. He was obviously concerned about her. But, more than that, it was what that concern had brought him face to face with. For he didn't want to simply sit there. He wanted to ask people if they had seen his granddaughter, tell people to look for her, call the security guards and the police ... But he found himself unable to do any of that, his inability to speak English weighing him down like a disability. He was trapped, trapped in his own foreignness, so much so that he was rendered powerless.

That was what she thought she saw in Ajay's face, as he stood there just inside the classroom door. She rose and walked up to him. At the time, she didn't know he was Indian. She thought he was an Arab. She spoke a smattering of Arabic. She thought she could help.

CHAPTER Thirty

That first day he dismissed her friendliness as a case of mistaken identity. After all, she did approach him in Arabic. The moment he finished telling her he was Indian, the professor arrived. He didn't see her after class. So he assumed she had simply mistaken him for someone else.

The next day, however, she came and sat next to him in class. After class, she asked him if he wanted to get some coffee.

He hesitated. He had another class to go to.

"It's no big deal," she said. "If you can't do it now we can do it some other time."

He made up his mind. What the hell ...

"No," he said. "Let's go."

She suggested an Italian coffee shop close to the campus. Although, he had never been to one before, he decided to go along with her. After all, how complicated could a cup of coffee get?

As they stood in line to order, however, he found himself gazing wide-eyed at the menu. The whole thing was Greek to him. He glanced at her, wondering whether he should ask her about the choices available. Then he rejected the idea. He didn't want her thinking he was ignorant. He figured he'd simply have whatever she was having.

When their turn to order came, however, she said she was still making up her mind. You go ahead, she told him. He swallowed. The woman, behind the cash register, smiled at him.

"What would you like to have, sir?" she asked.

He looked right and left, not knowing what to say. The woman waited. After a short pause, she said, "Do you need some time to make up your mind, sir?"

There was an edge to her voice and her smile was nowhere near as broad as when he had stepped up. The line, behind him, was getting restive as well.

"I think today's the day for a latte," Rose said to him. "What do you think?"

He nodded.

"How about two shots of vanilla to go with it?"

He nodded again.

She ordered two tall lattes with a couple of shots of vanilla. When they received their order, she looked on as he tasted his drink. When he nodded approvingly, she sighed, placing her hand on her chest in mock relief.

"You know that was my grandfather's favorite drink," she said. "He was from Lebanon. He liked his coffee sweet. That's why I would always add the vanilla."

"Well, I guess we Indians have a sweet tooth as well," he said.

They decided to sit near the window, at a square table flanked by two straight-backed chairs.

"Are you from Vancouver?" he asked her, once they were seated.

"No, I'm from Toronto. I've only been here three weeks."

"Well, that's two weeks more than what I can say."

They laughed. She opened her backpack and took out the class' syllabus and started scanning it.

"Have you bought your books yet?" she asked.

"No."

"This class is going to be tough on me," she said, with a shake of her head. "I just got a job in a bar. After closing up I don't get home until three in the morning. After that to get up for an eight'o clock class ..."

She sighed.

"Why don't you give up your job?" he said.

"Well, then who'll pay my rent?"

"But surely you have someone who can help you – a family member or some friend?'

"No, I'm all on my own."

He didn't know what to say to that. So he simply kept quiet and sipped his latte. She began to talk about the course, the professor, how full the classroom had been ... He told her about how strange it felt to be back in a classroom after more than fifteen years and, once again, listen to lectures and worry about homework. She asked him what he did in India. He said he worked for the government. When she inquired about his family, he simply said his wife was dead. He was glad she didn't ask any more personal questions.

They stayed in the coffee shop for almost an hour. Then she had to go. Reluctantly, he said goodbye to her. Then he went back to his room, where he lay down in bed and stared at the ceiling.

A single woman venturing into a new city to live her life entirely through her own devices. That was new for him. In his world, women didn't live by their own devices. Neither, for that matter, did men. You did not simply start a new life in a strange place. If you went anywhere, you went with your family. Or, conversely, you went to a place that was home to someone from your extended family. At the very least, you had a close friend there. You never ventured completely into the unknown ... Unless, of course, like him you were running away from something.

It was only later, when he had gotten to know her better, that he realized she too was on the run.

She was a dynamo. On most nights, she couldn't get to bed until three in the morning. Yet, unfailingly, she showed up for her eight'o clock class, looking like she'd slept her full eight hours. On the nights they stayed up to study for tests, it was invariably he who dropped off, stretching out on her living room carpet with a cushion for a pillow. When he woke up (or as she said "came to") she was still hard at work.

And this class is supposed to be tough on *you*, he said, with a rueful grin.

Around her, he felt vital, lively, light-headed ... As the days passed, he found himself living more and more for the time they spent together. On the days he didn't see her, he was miserable.

He told himself to snap out of it, finding several ways to explain away her interest in him. She was being polite; she was new in Vancouver and didn't know anyone else; she was curious about him because he was different ... Any day, he figured, she'd tire of being polite, or replace him with a new friend, or lose her curiosity in him ... After all, she was young and attractive. Quite a few men in the class itself were attracted to her; men that were younger and better-looking than him; men that were white like her ... So what chance did he stand – he – a middle-aged baggy-eyed Indian with graying hair?

Haven't you suffered enough already? he asked his reflection in the bathroom mirror.

CHAPTER
Thirty-one

One night, they sat up studying for a test on the carpet in Rose's tiny living room, quizzing each other on statistics over coffee and slices of pizza. The next day, after they were done with the test, Rose suggested they go for a movie in the evening. "I've got the night off," she said. "So let's make it a date."

That evening, at her behest, they went to see John Travolta in *Staying Alive.*

"So what do you think?" she asked him, after the movie, as they made their way to the parking lot.

"It was good," he said.

Actually, he had hated it.

"Really?" she said. "Well, I thought it was pretty awful. I think Stallone should stick to directing himself."

A little later, she asked, "Now tell me, did you really think it was good?"

"No, I actually hated it."

They both laughed. He glanced at her, thinking how lovely she looked. She was dressed simply in a pair of jeans and a white T-shirt. She had virtually no make-up on. Yet she stood out among all the women there. He had seen several men eyeing her. One or two had even eyed him enviously, which he had to admit made him feel good.

He looked at his watch. It wasn't even ten yet. The prospect of going back alone to his shoebox of a room depressed him.

"Can we go somewhere else?" he said, as they reached her car.

He spoke without thinking. The moment he finished he wished he hadn't spoken. Suppose she took it amiss ...

She unlocked her car and got in. He got in as well, feeling decidedly alarmed. He wondered if he should apologize. Maybe if he said ...

"You want to come over to my place," she said.

They were still in bed the next morning when he told her that last night had been his first date.

She propped herself up on one elbow and stared at him.

"You can't be serious," she said.

"I am."

"You mean you never dated anyone before?"

"No."

"Not even your *wife*?"

"No."

'Then how did the two of you get married?"

"A social worker at the orphanage where I grew up arranged it. He showed me her photograph. But I only saw her in person on the night we were married."

"So you fell in love with her *after* marriage?"

"Yes. I know it seems strange to you. But that's the way it happens in India."

She was quiet. Then, after a short pause, she said, "Your wife's been dead for over a year."

"Yes."

"And there's been no one since?"

"Not until last night."

One day, while standing in the hallway, waiting for one of her classes to end, he found himself marveling at his situation. Here he was at forty, a university student, waiting for his girl with the anticipation reserved for a first love. The thought made him smile. How different all that was from when he was actually eighteen. At eighteen, he had been poor. To make ends meet he had to work all day, which meant he could only attend classes at night. His abiding memory of those days was of the time he spent feeling spent. The vitality he felt now had been foreign to him.

Furthermore, at eighteen, he would have frowned at the kind of relationship he had with Rose. *A man and a woman involved with each other without being married.* He would have found the whole idea disturbing, even repugnant. Now, however, he was simply grateful.

What a stuffy old codger I was at eighteen, he thought, with a smile.

There seemed no end to the ways in which she could surprise him. Each time they made love, he discovered something new about her; a miniscule tattoo, the shape of a flower, on her back, a small scar – a vestige of a childhood prank gone awry – below the nape of her neck, a brown mole just above her navel ... A *brown* mole. The first time he saw it he stared. He had never seen a *brown* mole before. Chestnut hair, green eyes, now a *brown* mole ... Who said whites were not colored?

And then there were ways in which he surprised himself. He had never considered himself a possessive man. With Rose, however, he was frequently beset with jealousy. All she had to do was smile and talk to a man for a few minutes, and he found himself hating him. One time, when they ran into one of her professors at a cinema, she held the man's hand briefly and he spent the entire movie wondering whether they were having an affair. He only relaxed when she told him the man was gay.

You're so paranoid as if I were your wife, she said, laughing.

He didn't tell her he had never felt that way with his wife. No, with his wife it had been different. He and his wife had been two strangers bound by custom to spend the rest of their life together once they were married. The closeness they had come to share had developed slowly. He had grown to love his wife in increments, finding one more thing to love about her with each passing day.

No, with his wife possession had preceded love. Even though they had each other, it was months before they were at ease with one other. With Rose, however, he had found himself at ease within days.

Just how much Rose made him feel at ease, he figured out only after he'd spent a few months in Vancouver. By then, he had realized, no matter where he went, he was looked upon as a prototype. People quizzed him on India's poverty, overpopulation, spirituality ... He functioned variously as an encyclopedia, a guide, an interpreter, a sounding board ... He was conscious all the time whatever he said or did could form the basis of a generalization about hundreds of millions of people. It was only with Rose that he felt he could be himself – Ajay.

He marveled at how quickly he became intimate with her. He had never been a man who opened up easily to people. At four, he had lost both parents in the riots that accompanied partition. That early acquaintance with tragedy, coupled with the harshness of life in an orphanage, had forced him inward. As an adult, he had learned to conceal his remoteness, donning the armor of banter, cultivating the smiling face and the art of the backslap. Behind the sunny demeanor, however, remained a nature that found it difficult to trust; that revealed itself, even to close friends, in rare glimpses.

With Rose, however, before long he was sharing himself with the urgency of a man eager to be relieved of a punishing burden. At the moment, he didn't realize that he really wasn't acting that differently from most men that keep things locked up inside; that, unconsciously, all along he wished for nothing more than a confidante. His wife had fulfilled that role for several years. After her death, however, he'd had no one. With the result, once he opened up to Rose, he found he couldn't stop.

When he returned to India in the summer, friends, who hadn't seen him in nine months, found him more distant and preoccupied than ever before. Pritam wondered aloud if he was still thinking of his wife. Pritam's wife Simran shook her head, marveling at the foolishness of men. Yes, it was obvious Ajay had a woman on his mind, but one who was very much alive.

She wasn't in the least bit surprised when Ajay returned to Canada within a week, almost two months before expected.

CHAPTER
Thirty-two

His homecoming had been nothing he could have envisioned.

The melancholy exploded on him a few hours after he reached Delhi. In the beginning everything was okay. Pritam picked him up at the airport and drove him home, where the cook had dinner waiting and the houseboy stood ready to serve. At his request, Pritam stayed for dinner. After dinner, they moved to the drawing room where Pritam brought him up to date with what was going on at work over a cup of coffee. Then Pritam had to leave. He said goodbye to Pritam. Then he dismissed the servants for the night and settled in his study to wade through the mail that had piled up over the nine months he had been away.

By the time he was done, it was three in the morning – about two thirty yesterday afternoon on the West Coast. He wasn't in the least bit sleepy. With his body still on West Coast time, it was obvious sleep would be a long time coming. He decided to take a look at the rest of the house.

Everything was exactly where he had left it nine months ago; the furniture, the books, the pictures on the walls ... Yet the house appeared barer and emptier than ever before. As he went from room to room, he had the feeling that he was being swallowed deeper and deeper into the mouth of a dried-up well. Finally, he sank heavily into a chair. He wished he were far away from there. He wished he were back in Vancouver with Rose. He craved the sound of her voice, the touch of her lips, the garland of her arms round his neck ...

With a despairing sigh, he leaned back in his chair and closed his eyes. For a few minutes, he sat still with his eyes closed. Then he opened them to stare fixedly in front of him.

In a year, maybe two, when he had completed his course, he'd be back home for good, back in that house where he had plenty of people to order about, but only one person with whom to converse – himself.

He buried his face in his hands.

How little he actually knew Rose.

He knew she was the only child of divorced parents. Her father was Scotch-Canadian, while her mother had Lebanese ancestry. Both had remarried. Her father had moved down to Florida, while her mother still resided in Toronto. Rose herself had grown up in Toronto and lived there until the past year.

As a person, he knew her to be someone who abhorred ostentation. Her apartment was comfortable rather than luxurious. The gray Toyota she drove was strictly utilitarian. The clothes she wore were simple; she could spend days in a faded T-shirt and an old pair of jeans. She used very little makeup ... As far as food went, when he had first met her, she was living on salads and TV dinners. Since meeting him, however, she had acquired a taste for Indian food. In the last few weeks before he left for India, she had even begun to try her hand at making some of the dishes – something he had wished she wouldn't do since he was the one who had to first eat them and then muster up his most sincere face to tell her how good they were.

She was also one of the few people he had met in Canada who still read avidly; in fact, she read much more than she watched TV. She was the only person he knew who still read poetry. She could sit up all night discussing Yeats and the Celtic twilight. In a way, he found that somewhat surprising; the fact that she, who eschewed all ostentation in her own life, should be drawn to verse that was so ornate.

Yet, despite all that, when he really sat down and thought about it, he didn't think he knew her much better than a sketch. For instance, while he knew about her parents, he didn't know the nature of her relationship with them. He didn't think it was close. They rarely, if ever, came up in conversation. He couldn't remember her ever speaking to them over the phone or writing anything other than Christmas cards. But he couldn't begin to tell why she wasn't close to them or whether it had always been that way.

He realized how odd it was that, after practically living with a woman for seven months, he should know so little about her core. The truth, however, was that, in all the time they had spent together, he had been too busy exorcising himself from the past to spare a thought for anything else. Selfishly, he had squeezed her for comfort, while dumping on her the entire burden of his demons. Not once had he paused to look for wrinkles in her exterior. To put it plainly, he had been more of a patient than a lover.

And, maybe, towards the end she had tired of playing nurse. Maybe that was why she had behaved the way she did when he was leaving for India. He had expected tears from her. Instead, all he had gotten was silence. On the morning he was due to leave, she had simply hidden behind a pair of dark glasses and driven him to the airport without saying a word. In spite of his best efforts, she had refused to be drawn into a conversation. At the airport, she had kept her dark glasses on and buried her face in a magazine. When the call had come for him to board, she had said goodbye to him like an estranged sister, kissing him on the cheek almost as if she were fulfilling a ritual. Then she had turned and walked away, not even waiting for him to go aboard.

So would she want to spend the rest of her life with him? He couldn't say. But, at the very least, he had to make the effort. For if he had learned anything from the week he had spent in Delhi, it was that he couldn't live without her.

CHAPTER
Thirty-three

He was outside her front door.

The week of literally bullying his travel agent into getting him back to Vancouver as soon as possible, the mad dash across the world, the many hours spent thinking what to say to her ... It had all come down to that moment.

With a deep breath, he rang the doorbell. How would she react to seeing him? Would she be happy? Would she be indifferent? Or would she merely be surprised? ...

A moment crawled past, then another ... Still the front door didn't open. Again he rang the doorbell. It was only six in the morning. Quite possibly, she had heard the first ring and simply turned over in bed and gone back to sleep, hoping whoever it was would go away. Well, in that case, the second ring would convince her the person wasn't planning on going anywhere.

Thirty seconds passed, then a full minute, still no answer. He wondered if she had gone out. Then he remembered seeing her car in the parking lot on his way up.

For the third time, he pressed the doorbell. No sooner than the ring sounded, he heard her voice, thick with sleep, telling him that she was coming.

She opened the door with a yawn. Her eyes were all red and puffed up. Her hair was a mess. Her dressing gown was rumpled. On her feet she had a disparate pair of rubber slippers on – the right one red, the left one blue.

For him, however, there couldn't have been a more welcome sight. He swallowed. He had memorized an entire speech for that moment. Now, however, he couldn't recall a single word. All he could do was look at her.

It was she, who finally stepped forward, to fling her arms round his neck.

A few hours later, they were in bed, having just finished making love. She propped her head on her elbow and looked down at him.

"I've never missed anyone the way I missed you," she said. "I thought you were never coming back."

"I would've come sooner," he said. "Only all the flights were full."

She smiled and kissed him on the lips. He started to speak. She, however, placed a finger on his mouth.

"Just hold me," she said.

He put his arms round her and pulled her close. She lay with her head on his chest. Gently, he stroked her hair. Then, on impulse, he slid his hand down her back and squeezed her buttock. She bit him on the shoulder.

"Two can play at that," she said.

He laughed. For the first time in days, he felt alive. He had an insane desire to jump up and down, shouting like an idiot. He couldn't recall a moment in his life where he had been happier. He closed his eyes, soaking in the feeling. For the next few minutes, he was content to simply lie there and let it wash all over him. Then he opened his eyes and said, "Rose."

There was no answer. She had fallen asleep. Gently, he disentangled his arms and legs from hers, taking care not to wake her up. Then he kissed her lightly on the top of her head and placed the sheet over her.

With a sigh, he lay back on his side of the bed. All of a sudden, he felt tired. The jet lag was finally catching up with him. He glanced at the radio clock, placed on the table beside the bed. It was almost ten thirty in the morning, close to eleven in the night in Delhi. Bedtime.

He closed his eyes, thinking he'd talk to her about the future when she woke up. In light of everything that had happened so far that morning, however, he was more than optimistic. For the first time, he believed everything was going to turn out fine.

Secure in that belief, he went to sleep.

He woke up to find himself alone in bed. A note, lying on the table beside the bed, informed him that she had gone to work. It went on to say that there was food in the fridge, in case he got hungry, and that she'd be home by three.

That meant she wouldn't be home for another three hours, he reasoned. For it was just past midnight.

He rose and put on his shirt and underpants and went into the kitchen. There he found half a pizza in the fridge. He heated it up in the microwave and ate a late dinner of pizza and coke. By the time he was finished, it was twelve thirty. He decided to change into his nightclothes. They were, however, in his suitcases which he still had to unpack. He tried to recall where he had put his suitcase keys. On the plane, he had carried them in a small black pouch that he kept in his trousers pockets. As far as he could remember, he had placed the pouch on Rose's dining table in the morning. The dining table, however, was now empty. And there was no sign of the pouch in the kitchen or the living room either.

He went into the bedroom. For a moment, he hesitated, wondering whether he should look in Rose's dresser. Then he shrugged his shoulders. What the hell ... He was sure she wouldn't mind.

He didn't find the pouch in the two top drawers. In the third drawer from the top, however, he found something that made him forget the pouch altogether.

Lying there, among a bunch of old sweaters, was a picture of Rose with a man – a tall slim man in his late thirties or early forties. He was evidently athletic; his narrow waist and broad shoulders attested to that. The glasses he wore, however, gave him an intellectual air. His straight dark hair, though graying at the temples, was still thick and fell forward on his forehead in a wave. He had a square jaw, a full mouth, a long thin nose and large brown eyes. Clearly, he was handsome.

He was standing with his arm round Rose. From the way he was holding her, it was obvious they were lovers. From the way she was looking at him, it was apparent she was in love.

CHAPTER
Thirty-four

He was out on the balcony when she returned to the apartment complex. He watched her park the car. She was still standing outside the front door, fumbling in her handbag for her keys, when he yanked the front door open. No sooner than she'd stepped inside, he thrust the photograph in her hands and fired off a burst of questions. Who was the man with her in the picture? How did she come to meet him? Was she still seeing him? ...

She sank on to the living room couch. She was aching all over. That night work had been hell. One of the other girls had called in sick at the last minute, leaving them shorthanded, that too on a Friday night. With the result, by the time the bar closed, everyone was exhausted.

She'd had trouble keeping her eyes open on the drive home. She was dying to kick off her shoes and collapse in bed. She was sure she'd fall asleep even before her head hit the pillow.

But with Ajay pacing about, practically foaming at the mouth ... She took a deep breath.

"His name was Richard Green," she said.

He stopped pacing and turned to her.

"I met him three years ago when I was a junior at the University of Toronto. He was my professor. He taught English.

"He was also married.

"I was just returning to school. I had dropped out when I was twenty to move in with my boyfriend, Nathan. For two years I was a full-time live-in girlfriend. One day Nathan simply came home and told me it was over. He had met this other girl a few months ago. He said he was in love with her and they were going to get married.

"I didn't know what to do. For two years my life had revolved round him. Now I was left on my own with nowhere to go. I had very little money. So I had no choice except to move back in with Mother, which was awful. Mother had remarried. I felt like an intruder in the house. The fact I didn't get along with my stepfather didn't help matters ... My own father I hadn't seen in years. He lived down in Florida and other than the occasional letter or phone call we had very little contact.

"So I was feeling very much on my own as I started to pick up the pieces of my life. Outwardly I put up a brave front. I registered for classes at the university; I got up every morning and went to school; I even got a job on campus ... Inside, however, I was anything but together. I felt abandoned; I was scared ... I guess that's where Richard came in. I needed a shoulder to lean on, and he was there to offer his.

"It started innocently enough. Having been out of school for two years I had fallen out of the habit of studying or doing homework. In the beginning I found the going especially tough. Frequently I needed help. So I would go to talk to Richard in his office. Unlike the other professors, he was very accessible. Then he had the knack of putting you at ease. Many times I went to him completely out of sorts to leave feeling much more positive, even optimistic.

"At first we only discussed coursework. It didn't take long, however, for things to get personal. Pretty soon I was telling him about Nathan and myself, about how lonely I felt in the wake of our break-up, about how awkward it was to be living at home again

... I was seeing him practically every day, sometimes for hours. We would have lunch together. Then he'd drive me home ... In a few short weeks he had ceased to be my teacher. He had become more of a friend, a confidante.

"Then one day he asked me to spend the weekend with him. His wife and daughter were going out of town. We had the entire weekend to ourselves. I guess I should have said no. By then, however, I was in love with him."

She paused. Ajay was no longer looking at her. He was sitting, with his hands clasped together, staring at the wall in front of him. When she stopped talking, he didn't react, simply continued to stare straight ahead, with his face just as impassive as before.

She continued.

"It wasn't much. A weekend here, a stolen afternoon, a fuck in a motel room ... Mere crumbs. But when you have nothing you can live a long time on crumbs. For months it didn't matter to me that he wasn't mine, that I was little more than an extra in his life, that at the end of it all he would go back home to his wife ... I was simply happy with whatever I could get.

"No one, however, can live on crumbs forever. Finally, it became too much for me. I got sick of the lying; of sneaking about like a thief; more than anything, of having to share him with his wife and family. So I went up to him and told him I couldn't keep on going like that any longer. I loved him and couldn't bear to be apart from him. I wanted us to be together. I wanted to get married.

"He said he felt the same way. However, he couldn't just get up and walk out on his wife. They had been married a long time. Then they had a daughter. He needed time, a few months at least.

"I agreed to wait. I guess I should have realized then that he never intended to leave his wife and daughter. But at the time I wanted him so much; I was willing to believe anything in order to get him.

"The weeks passed, then months. Richard showed no sign of

getting a divorce. Rather, he started seeing less of me. He also started going out of town a lot. He said he was going to conferences and presenting papers when, in actual fact, he was interviewing. He had applied to a number of colleges and universities and chances were he would soon be leaving Toronto.

"I learned that quite by accident. I was looking through a schedule of next fall's classes and couldn't find his name anywhere. So I went to ask in the department. The department head told me that Richard had informed him he wasn't returning next year.

"Now I was really desperate. I was losing Richard and I had no idea how I would go on without him."

She hesitated. Then she said, in a low voice, "That's when I stopped taking the pill."

Ajay turned towards her. She continued, gazing fixedly in front of her, "Soon I had my wish. I tested myself twice to make sure. Then I marched off to tell Richard.

"He reacted the way I should have expected, saying in as many words what his actions had said for months. He made it plain that he wasn't ready to leave his wife and daughter. He had gotten a job in Ottawa and would be moving soon. He said it was for the best, something I would realize in time. In the meanwhile, the best thing for me to do was to get an abortion. He was prepared to help in any way he could.

"I was flabbergasted. I stood and stared at him, unable to believe my ears. It was the last thing I expected. Now when I look back on it, I wonder how I could have expected anything else. The writing was there on the wall. But I had closed my eyes to reality for so long it was jarring to have them opened so abruptly. I screamed at Richard. I said I wasn't going to let him get away with it, that I would go straight out and tell his wife, that I would ruin his entire life ... I don't know for how long I ranted and raved. I was mad.

"I stomped out on him that day. But I never went to his wife as I had promised. In fact, I didn't tell anybody. Once I was alone, the anger subsided quickly. I started to cry, I don't know for how long. Even after I ran out of tears, I continued crying inside. My mind was like a maelstrom, with all sorts of thoughts crashing inside my head. It was a long time before I calmed down enough to think straight. When I did, the overwhelming feeling was not one of anger or sorrow, but disappointment. I was disappointed in Richard, disappointed in losing everything we could have had together

... But, more than anything, I was disappointed in myself. Once again I had boxed myself into a situation where I would have to start over and pick up the pieces of my life. This time, I promised myself, that I'd do a better job. Instead of looking to others, I'd put my faith in the only person I could count on – myself.

"I made up my mind to leave Toronto. There was nothing to hold me there. Mother was getting on with her life. All my friends were busy with theirs. And, anyway, I wanted to start with a clean slate, which I didn't think was possible in Toronto.

"I was due to graduate in a few months. I decided to go for my master's degree. I applied to various programs. The University of British Columbia accepted me. So I came here.

"However, even after the way he acted, it was a long time before I truly got over Richard. I told myself I hated him. But I did not. I still don't. I simply don't love him any more. I haven't looked at that photograph of his in months – not once since I met you. In fact, I don't even remember where I'd put it."

She was quiet. There was a short pause. Then Ajay asked, "What happened to the child?"

"I got an abortion. One day after classes I went to a clinic. By the evening I was home, doing homework. At the time I told myself I got the abortion because I wanted no part of Richard. The real reason, however, was that I was not ready to be a mother. I had gotten pregnant for all the wrong reasons.

"Now, however, there are times I wonder what if I'd had the baby. When I see other people's babies outgrowing their clothes and learning to walk and speaking their first words ... I tell myself my baby would be ready for this now, or that. Then I realize I don't even know whether it was a boy or a girl."

Tears sprang in her eyes. She took out her handkerchief and started drying them. Ajay came over and put his arm round her.

"Come on," he said. "It's late and you must be tired. Let's go to bed."

"No, there is something I have to tell you."

"You can tell me in the morning."

"No, I must tell you now.

"The day before you left for India I did a pregnancy test. I had missed a period and was getting bouts of morning sickness. So I wanted to make sure.

"The test came out positive.

"I didn't tell you. You were going home. I didn't know if you were coming back. I very much doubted it. After all, you came over here to get over your wife and, as far as I could see, you had gotten over her. And, anyway, I wasn't ready to make the same mistake again. Not because I thought you'd act like Richard. No, I knew you could be counted on to do the honorable thing. But that wasn't the way I wanted you. I was sick of making do with crumbs. I didn't want any more.

"So I decided I'd tell you if you came back. Otherwise I'd raise the child on my own. It was hard, however, on that last morning. So many times I was tempted to tell you for no other reason than to stop you from going. I was scared that if I opened my mouth I'd blurt it out sooner or later. So I decided to keep my mouth shut the whole time. I know you were a little put off by that. I'm sorry. But I couldn't help it."

She was finished. He didn't say anything. Even with all the surprises that had befallen him that night, it was obvious he wasn't ready for something like that

She leaned back and closed her eyes. She was utterly spent. If only she could sit with her eyes closed for a moment ...

That was the last thought she had before she fell asleep.

CHAPTER
Thirty-five

When she woke up, she was still on the living room couch. However, she was lying down. She still had her jeans and T-shirt on. Her shoes, however, were off and lay next to the couch. There was also a cushion placed underneath her head and a blanket on top of her. She had no memory of either taking off her shoes or getting the cushion and blanket. For that matter, she had no memory of falling asleep.

She must have dropped off soon after telling Ajay she was pregnant. She had been so fatigued after she stopped talking. She had leaned back and closed her eyes, thinking she'd open them in a moment. Instead, she must have fallen asleep. Ajay must have taken her shoes off and laid her down and put the blanket on top of her.

Ajay. Where was he? She sat up and called out his name. He didn't answer. She threw a quick glance at the far corner of the living room where his bags had stood the night before. They were nowhere to be seen. For one wrenching instant, she thought he'd left. Then she spotted him through the glass sliding doors. He was out on the balcony. He must have done some unpacking last night. For he was dressed in a cream-colored kurta-pajama.

She got up and walked over to the sliding doors. Before opening them, however, she hesitated.

What would he be like now that he knew everything?

With a deep breath, she slid the doors open and stepped out on to the balcony. Outside, it was more dawn than morning. The street below was quiet. And the sky looked as if it had been spraypainted in various shades of red, pink and orange.

Ajay turned and put his arms round her waist.

"Let's get married," he said.

The Monster at Rest

CHAPTER
Thirty-six

"Ramesh," Jaswant spoke into the phone, "Ramesh, this is Jaswant. Can you hear me?

"Good. Did you get anything on Ajay Ahuja?"

For the next few minutes, he listened in silence to the voice on the other end of the receiver. Then he thanked Ramesh and said goodbye. After hanging up, he turned to Deepak and Amrita, who were waiting impatiently.

"Ajay Ahuja was forced to take early retirement from the RAW after Mrs. Gandhi's assassination," he said. "He retired to his house in Delhi and became a virtual recluse. In 1986, however, he and his wife left for a trip to Vancouver. Only the wife came back, and that too to simply sell the house and everything in it. Soon after that she returned to Canada. Neither she nor Ahuja have been back since."

"They might still be in Vancouver," Deepak said.

"Even if they were, how would we find them?" Amrita asked.

Jaswant opened the phone book.

'That wouldn't do any good," Amrita said. "There must be at least fifty Ahujas in there. Surely we can't call all of them?"

"We can't," Deepak said. "But there can't be that many Ajay Ahujas."

Amrita shrugged her shoulders. "It's a fairly common Indian name," she said.

"Come here," Jaswant said.

They went over.

"I was going through the list of Ahujas," he said. "And look what I found. It's the only one."

With his finger he zeroed in on a name in the phone book—Rose Ahuja.

Amrita slowed the car down to a crawl. The rain was coming down harder. It was dark as well. With the result, it was that much more difficult to make out the numbers of the houses drifting past to the right and left. In fact, she was almost past the house she wanted when Jaswant, seated behind her, said, "Stop, this is it."

She stopped and looked out the window.

"Are you sure?" she asked.

"Yes, this is it all right," Deepak, who was seated beside her in the passenger seat, said.

He pointed out the number on the mailbox. Amrita switched off the ignition and took a deep breath.

"Let's go," Deepak said.

He started to get out of the car.

"Wait," Amrita said.

He paused and turned to her.

"This is something I have to do on my own," she said.

"What are you saying, Amrita?" Jaswant said. "You can't go in there by yourself. In that house there is someone who killed your parents. You don't know what that person could do to you."

"I know that," Amrita said. "But you must understand – I have to do this on my own. Thirteen years ago I ran away from it. I thought that was the way to make a new beginning. All I've really been doing, however, is running. And I'm going to continue running until I face up to it and put every one of those old ghosts to rest. And only I can do it. This is no longer about Mrs. Gandhi or Khalistan. This is about me and my life."

She looked at Deepak. "You understand," she said.

He didn't answer.

"You're not going to let her go in there on her own," Jaswant said.

Deepak opened the car door and got out and walked round to the driver's side to open Amrita's door.

"We'll wait right here," he said to Amrita. "At the first sign of trouble scream your head off and we'll be in there."

Amrita nodded and stepped out of the car and began walking to the front door. The house was a single-story red brick house, with a small garden out front. A narrow graveled walkway ran beside the garden to the front door. Amrita went up the walkway and rang the doorbell. Presently the door opened.

A middle-aged woman stood in front of her. A slim woman, with pale dry skin and an angular face made severe by a short haircut and a pair of glasses. She was dressed in faded jeans and a wrinkled white T-shirt.

"Hello, Rose," Amrita said.

CHAPTER
Thirty-seven

She was sixteen again. She was at the Taj Mahal in Agra with her parents and Ajay Uncle and Ajay Uncle's new wife, whom she still hadn't gotten used to calling Rose Aunty. Dressed in a yellow salwar kameez, she was seated on a white marble bench between Rose and her mother. All three of them were watching her father try to talk a family out of having their lunch at a particular spot in a bid to secure the best possible backdrop for a picture he wanted to take of his friend Ajay and his new wife. Quite clearly, things were not going too well. The people were arguing and voices were raised.

Ajay had his hand on Pritam's arm. Obviously, he wanted no part of this. He spoke to Pritam, suggesting that maybe they should take their picture elsewhere. Pritam, however, refused to be dissuaded. A few minutes later, his persistence paid off, as the family started picking up their things.

Rose turned to Amrita and said, laughing, "Your father believes in sticking to his guns."

Amrita responded with a shy smile. It was over a week since she first met Rose. Yet she continued to feel awkward in her presence. Not that Rose hadn't been friendly or forthcoming. It was just that she was different from anyone Amrita had known her entire life.

She recalled the day she first met Rose. She had spent the entire day wondering how she should greet her. Should she kiss her on the cheek or shake hands, as she had seen women do in Hollywood films? Or should she stick to folding her hands and saying namaste?

She had continued to wonder right up to the moment that she actually met Rose. It was Rose who took matters out of her hands by giving her a hug.

Now, ten days later, she watched, as Rose posed for a photograph with her husband with the facade of the Taj Mahal as their backdrop. She marveled at her poise. Rose didn't look like a woman who had been in a foreign country for only two weeks. She appeared completely relaxed. Even the fact that she got stared at wherever she went, because she was white, didn't seem to faze her in the slightest. She even carried the sari off with aplomb. Looking at her, you wouldn't believe she was wearing it for the first time.

Pritam, peering through the camera lens, shouted, "Smile." Ajay and Rose obliged. Pritam held up one hand, telling them to be still. A little later, the camera clicked.

"Do you remember that picture?" Rose asked Amrita.

They were back in a suburban living room in Vancouver, thirteen years later. The picture hung on the wall in front of them in a gilt-edged frame.

Amrita nodded.

"The sari was your mother's idea," Rose said. "She said it would go wonderfully with Ajay's Jodhpuri coat. She especially went and got a red brocaded sari. She said I was on my honeymoon and so I should look like a bride. I must admit I was a little hesitant. I had never worn a sari before. I didn't even know how to tie one on. Your mother was the one who showed me. She dressed me up. She also showed me how to carry it off."

Smiling, she shook her head. "I guess I was like any Westerner going to India for the first time," she said. "The first thing I wanted to see was the Taj Mahal. I was so excited when I learned it was only two hundred kilometers from Delhi. 'Let's just drive up there on Saturday morning,' I said to Ajay. 'We'll be there in a couple of hours. We can spend the day there, then find a motel for the night.' He simply laughed. Of course that was before I learned about Indian roads and motels.

"However, Ajay did get your father to arrange the visit. He also asked your entire family to come along. That week we all spent in Agra was one of the best of my life."

She gazed at the picture a little longer. Then she turned away with a sigh.

"Won't you sit down," she said to Amrita.

Amrita settled in an overstuffed chair.

"I was just making myself a cup of tea," Rose said. "Would you like some?"

"Okay."

Rose left to get the tea. While she was gone, Amrita looked round, seeing other things in the room that were just as familiar as the picture – the Persian carpet with the floral design, the red divan across the room, the silver figurine of Nataraja, dancing in his circle of fire, on one of the shelves of the entertainment center ...

Rose returned with the tea. She handed Amrita a cup. Then she sat down on the divan.

"So how did you find me?" she asked.

Amrita told her. When she was finished, there was a short pause. Then Rose said, "What do you want?"

Amrita leaned forward.

"I have learned a lot today," she said. "Now after thirteen years I know that my parents were murdered. I also know the man responsible for their murder was my father's best friend. That's a lot to learn in one day. As I was driving up here, I was thinking maybe I should turn around and come back another day, give myself a few days to get used to everything I now know. But I couldn't do that. This has waited long enough and I am sick of all the lies. I want to know what actually happened. I want to know the whole truth."

As she finished, the door to the living room was flung open. A boy ran in; a boy of twelve, maybe thirteen, dressed in a pair of black shorts and a red jersey with the number 9 printed on the back in white. On his feet, he had soccer boots on. His muddy boots and damp clothes and disheveled hair suggested he'd come home directly from a game.

"Mom," he shouted, as he surged towards Rose.

Then he realized his mother had a visitor. He halted on his tracks, looking sheepish.

"I'm sorry," he mumbled.

Amrita looked askance.

"This is my son, Ajay," Rose said to her. "Ajay, this is Miss Gill."

"How do you do, Miss Gill," the boy said.

He started to shake hands. Then he stopped, realizing his hands were dirty.

Amrita stared at him. He had his mother's fair skin. Other than that, however, he was the spitting image of his father. He had the same straight black hair, the same black eyes, the same broad nose and thrusting chin ... even the same name.

"Why don't you go upstairs and take a shower," Rose said to him.

The boy turned to leave, obviously glad to be excused, only to turn around as he remembered his manners.

"It was very nice to meet you, Miss Gill," he said.

Amrita nodded. The boy left, closing the door behind him. After he was gone, Rose said, in a quiet voice, "Whatever we did, we did for him."

CHAPTER
Thirty-eight

"It was Ajay who insisted that we go to India right after we got married," Rose said. "He was bursting with all kinds of plans for the future. He wanted to repaint the house, do up the nursery, bring in new furniture ... He couldn't wait to get started.

"I was hesitant. I knew what he was getting at. He wanted the very best for our child and me. And he could only give us that in India, where he was well-established and had a good job waiting for him. What could he do for us here in Canada, where he was merely a middle-aged foreign student?

"For me, however, moving to India meant I had to leave my country and go live in a place about which I knew next to nothing. Therefore, I hesitated. Ajay, however, was persistent. Finally, I gave in. Under the circumstances, I had to agree what he had in mind was the best for our child.

"Within a week after we landed in India, Ajay had painters and builders in to do up the house. He put me in consultation with a doctor. He even began buying toys for the baby. One day I remember him coming home with a popgun. I asked him how he could be so sure the kid would like it. He said that of course the kid would. He could vouch for that since it was what he'd liked when he was a kid himself. I asked what if the kid was a girl. He had no answer to that. The next day, however, he came home with an armful of dolls.

"He was the perfect father-in-waiting. Maybe too perfect, considering he wouldn't let me do a thing. He insisted on fetching and carrying for me, that too in a country where a wife is supposed to be at her husband's beck and call. There were actually people that wondered if he wasn't a bit touched by the sun.

"We were so happy in those days. We had each other, a child to look forward to, a nice big house, enough money ... Things couldn't have been more perfect.

"Everything, however, changed after Mrs. Gandhi sent the army into the Golden Temple.

"Until then, Ajay had worked banker's hours. Sometimes not even that. He wanted to take care of me, show me as much of India as he possibly could. He took me to Agra, then Shimla and

Jaipur. It was wonderful.

"After the army raided the Golden Temple, however, work piled up on him. He began to work late. He had meetings that went well into the night. He also started bringing work home. When he was home, he was frequently on the phone, requesting information, passing orders, issuing instructions ...

"He couldn't help it. The entire intelligence community was up in arms. Memos were flying all over the place, as people parceled out blame for the fact that the army had not received complete information on the strength of the Golden Temple defenses. As a result, there had been heavy casualties, turning what was supposed to be a quick surgical strike into a long drawn-out bloody mess.

"It was in those circumstances that Pritam requested a meeting with Ajay. Pritam was concerned that everyone was so busy pointing fingers they were losing sight of the real problem. By sending the army into the Golden Temple, Mrs. Gandhi had created more Sikh militants in one night than militant leaders could have hoped for after years of indoctrination. Many Sikhs, who had never expected to have anything to do with Khalistan, would now be joining up in droves. The militant was no longer merely the religious fanatic, the petty criminal looking for loot, the unemployed peasant ... Now he could be anybody. He could even be someone with access to the prime minister. And whoever he was, now he had only one goal in mind – kill Indira Gandhi. True, many spur-of-the-moment militants would fizzle out once the anger had passed and reality set in. But even one new hardcore militant, who remained unidentified, was one too many. For it was an unequal fight, where the assassin had the upper hand; he only had to get lucky once.

"Ajay accepted what Pritam was saying. He asked him what he proposed to do. Pritam said, first and foremost, they needed more sources of information in Delhi's gurudwaras. Militants used the gurudwaras to hide out from the police. Furthermore, that was where new militants were recruited, strategies for future militant attacks were chalked out, weapons and ammunition were stored ... The gurudwaras had to be priority number one.

"Ajay agreed. He entrusted Pritam with the responsibility of setting up a network of agents, informers and infiltrators that would keep them updated on the goings-on inside the gurudwaras. To minimize the chance for leaks, he had Pritam report directly to him. He didn't want to take a chance with go-betweens. In fact, he didn't want anyone, except Pritam and himself, to know what they were doing. The militants had sympathetic elements within the intelligence community, and Ajay wanted to minimize the risk of them ever finding out.

"About ten days after they talked, Pritam received some pictures of new militants, that had been recruited by one of Delhi's militant groups, from one of his agents. For the most part, they were poor disaffected Sikh youths. One of them, however, caught Pritam's eye; a boy of about twenty called Harkishan who, according to the agent's report, had an uncle in government service. On further investigation, Pritam learned the Uncle's name was Gurbachan Singh and he was the boy's only living relative. He also learned that Gurbachan was in the DGS and D and spent a lot of his time in the Bangla Sahib gurudwara.

"The Bangla Sahib was close to the prime minister's residence. It was also a hotbed of militant activity. So, while Pritam had all the other new militants arrested, he held off on arresting Harkishan. First he wanted to have a talk with Gurbachan.

"What Pritam had in mind was simple. He would tell Gurbachan that he'd sit on Harkishan's file as long as Gurbachan gave him reports of what was going on inside the Bangla Sahib. If Gurbachan refused to cooperate, then he'd have Harkishan picked up for treason.

"He put that proposition directly to Gurbachan when they met. Gurbachan, of course, had no alternative but to comply. However, even Pritam did not realize how useful a source Gurbachan Singh was until he learned of his association with Beant Singh. He went straight to Ajay with that information. Right off the bat, the two of them knew they had dynamite. One of Mrs. Gandhi's bodyguards, a man who accompanied her everywhere, even abroad, was meeting with individuals who wanted to kill her! Ajay acted immediately. He passed the information on to his higher-ups who, in turn, fed it to those responsible for the P.M.'s security. Overnight, Beant Singh was transferred.

"Mrs. Gandhi, however, intervened and had the orders revoked. Beant Singh had been with her for years. She trusted him. She wanted to see solid proof of his disloyalty before she was willing to let him go. That Ajay and Pritam did not have.

"So Ajay told Pritam to keep close tabs on Beant Singh and update him regularly on his activities. That was the most they could do under the circumstances. However, he did tell Pritam that, if he so much as got a hint from his agent that Mrs. Gandhi was going to be harmed in any way, he was to tell him immediately.

"Three months later on October 30th, Pritam learned from Gurbachan Singh that Beant Singh planned to assassinate Mrs. Gandhi.

"He called Ajay immediately at his office. Ajay, however, had already left. So Pritam tried him at home. He wasn't there either. However, Pritam spoke to one of the servants, who told him that I had gone into labor and had been taken to the Escorts Hospital. Ajay had rushed there directly from work.

"Under normal circumstances, Pritam would have gone straight to the hospital. But, as you well know, he wasn't well that day. So he sat down and wrote a letter, detailing everything he had learned from Gurbachan Singh. He marked it personal and confidential. Sensing how important the information was, he decided against using one of the RAW's couriers. There had been several leaks over the past few months, and that was one letter he could not risk falling in the wrong hands. Therefore, he decided to send Tapan, one of his trusted servants, to the hospital with instructions to deliver the letter personally to Ajay.

"When Tapan reached the hospital, however, I was in a bad way. The baby was premature. It was only my eighth month. The labor pains were killing me. I needed Ajay on my side to keep going. So Tapan had to wait."

Amrita could see how that could have happened. Of course, if it had been her father in Tapan's place, that would never have happened. Her father would have simply flashed his VIP credentials and demanded to see Ajay immediately, irrespective of Rose's condition. But her father was a well-educated member of the city's elite. Tapan, on the other hand, was a simple man of little education who had done the bidding of his betters his entire life. In the hallways of one of Delhi's most exclusive private hospitals, he would have been intimidated by the sight of so many sahibs and memsahibs. With the result, when told to wait, he would have squatted meekly on the floor.

Rose, in the meanwhile, continued.

"It was a long time before Ajay could dash off to see Tapan, that too only for a minute – just long enough for him to take the letter, stash it away in his pockets and hurry back to me. He thought he'd read it the first chance he got. That night, however, he never got that chance. He only read it the next morning. That night, while caring for his wife and helping her give birth to the child he'd always wanted, he forgot all about the letter. It was only in the morning, after his son had been born and he was assured that both mother and child were safe, that he remembered it. Upon reading it, he ran to the nearest phone. But he was too late. Mrs. Gandhi had already been shot."

CHAPTER
Thirty-nine

"Ajay was stunned by the news of Mrs. Gandhi's shooting and subsequent death," Rose said. "It took him a while to recover from the shock. Once he did, however, it wasn't long before he recognized the gravity of his situation.

"He was staring early retirement squarely in the eye. Heads were bound to roll in the intelligence community now that the prime minister had been shot. However, if it ever came out that he'd had the information to save her on his person for more than twelve hours before the assassination and done nothing with it, he was looking at a whole lot worse. For starters, he'd lose his pension. Then he'd be accused of treason, and many people would assume he was guilty. Who would believe that someone in his position could forget about such an important letter just because he was helping his wife give birth to their son? Only people who knew Ajay well knew what that child meant to him. In such an event, he'd lose whatever face he had left, as well as the respectability and social position he had spent a lifetime building.

"In that scenario, what kind of life could he offer his wife and newborn son?

"But wait a minute. Wait. Maybe all wasn't lost just yet. Maybe there was still a chance. After all, who knew he had known anything about the plot to assassinate Mrs. Gandhi? Only Pritam and Gurbachan, as far as he could tell. Now, as far as Gurbachan was concerned, he knew enough about him to know he could be bought. With his penchant for petty bribes, Gurbachan was often called Mr. Cash Register by his colleagues at the DGS and D. Pritam, however, was a different matter altogether. Pritam wouldn't sell his silence, no matter what the price. But Pritam was his dearest friend, practically a brother. Pritam knew everything he had gone through. And now that he had rebuilt his life, surely Pritam wouldn't bring the house down.

"So it was with the utmost confidence that Ajay went to Pritam's house. Pritam was back on his feet, although he was still moving about with some difficulty. He was busy making arrangements to send you and your mother to Amritsar on the night train. Now that

Mrs. Gandhi had been killed by two Sikhs, he feared a backlash against Sikhs in Delhi. So he wanted to get you and your mother out of all possible danger.

"The moment they were alone, Ajay explained what had happened. He was sure that, once he had put matters in perspective, Pritam would see things his way. To his shock, however, he found that Pritam saw them very differently.

"Pritam agreed that heads were bound to roll now that they had lost the prime minister. But his head wasn't going to be one of them. As far as he was concerned, he had done his job and that was exactly what he was going to tell the world. It wasn't that he didn't want to help Ajay. But he couldn't afford to lose his job. He had a family to support, a daughter to marry off ... Furthermore, he was a Sikh. Now that two Sikhs had shot Mrs. Gandhi, every Sikh was bound to be viewed with suspicion. It was highly likely that if he said he knew nothing about the plot to assassinate Mrs. Gandhi, some people might interpret his ignorance as calculated treason rather than simple negligence. So, while he sympathized with Ajay, he simply couldn't afford to take the risk. He had a family to think of.

"Ajay couldn't believe his ears. It was the last thing he could have expected. He reminded Pritam of how long they had been friends, of the years they had spent together – first in the police and then in the intelligence, even of the times that he – Ajay – had gone out of his way for Pritam ... Finally, he begged Pritam to think of his newborn son. What kind of life could he give his son if he lost everything ... It all got pretty emotional. At one point, both men were in tears. But, despite it all, Pritam remained adamant.

"By the time he left Pritam's house, Ajay was shaken. The irony was simply too much for him. He had lost everything on the same day that he had gotten everything he had ever wanted. He drove about aimlessly, not really caring where he was going. When he couldn't go any further, he parked the car next to the kerb and slumped forward on the wheel.

"The thirty minutes or so, that had elapsed between the birth of his son and the moment where he recalled the letter from Pritam, filled his mind. He couldn't remember another time in his life where he had felt more fulfilled, more at peace with himself, more optimistic about the future ... All the things that had gone wrong in the past had been wiped out. He had been freed of all regrets. Now he could simply live and savor each one of the gifts that life had bestowed upon him.

"At that moment, however, all that appeared to have been a mirage.

"Then it struck him that it did not have to be so. After all, the only person standing in his way was Pritam. If Pritam were somehow ... He dismissed the thought. A few minutes later, however, it returned. And this time it refused to go away. A plan began to take shape. Already gangs of hooligans were roaming the streets. Ajay had seen them pull Sikhs out of cars and buses and attack them with machetes and steel rods. As the day wore, such attacks were bound to escalate. Pritam was a Sikh. If he were to be found murdered that day, the first conclusion anyone would draw was that he had fallen prey to some vengeful Hindu fanatic.

"The more he thought about it, the more feasible the idea seemed. You and your mother were leaving for Amritsar that night. So Pritam would be alone at home, which was just fine. Not for a moment did Ajay want to hurt you or your mother. The train for Amritsar left at nine thirty. It was an hour's drive from your house to the railway station. That meant, to be on that train, you and your mother had to leave for the station by eight at the latest. So if Ajay went to the house round eight thirty, Pritam was bound to be alone. By then, any servant who had shown up for work that day would have been dismissed for the night. And the fact it would be dark would allow Ajay to get in and out of the house without being noticed. Not that Ajay foresaw any problems getting in. He figured all he had to do was knock on the front door. He was sure Pritam would let him in. There had been tears in Pritam's eyes when they had parted that morning. It was obvious Pritam was feeling guilty. Certainly he wasn't going to add to that guilt by turning him away at the door.

"Once he was inside, he'd do it the first chance he got. He'd get Pritam from behind with a rope, which would make far less noise than a gun. Pritam wouldn't be expecting an attack. So he wouldn't have time to react, especially to an assailant from behind him. The fact he'd still be nursing the after effects of a twisted ankle would restrict him further. After Pritam was dead, he would ransack the house to make it look like it had been looted. To make the scenario more believable, he'd take whatever money and jewelry he could lay his hands on. With the dead body, the things strewn all over the floor, the missing money and jewelry ... who would conclude that this was any different from countless other attacks that were being carried out against Sikhs and their property all over Delhi?

"He went over the plan in his mind several times. It appeared sound. He seemed to have catered for everything.

"The question, however, was – could he do it? He hadn't killed anyone in years. Not since he was a junior police officer. And those people had been gangsters, dacoits, drug traffickers ... Pritam was his friend.

"But then, again, Pritam wasn't acting like a friend. He had left him no choice. He had to do it. Once again, he went over the plan. It was perfect.

"That night, however, things went horribly wrong. As it turned out, your father wasn't alone. Your mother had stayed back with him. And Ajay didn't find that out until it was too late. He had already killed your father and finished emptying out the closets and almirahs to make it look as if a gang of hooligans had gone through the place, when your mother stepped out of the bathroom in her nightgown. She had been taking her nightly bath. When she saw Ajay, she screamed. Ajay reacted instantly. He took out his gun and shot her right between the eyes.

"On any other night, that shot would have brought people running. But it wasn't any other night. Everyone knew what was going on in the city that night. So the neighbors waited. Nobody was willing to venture out until they were absolutely sure it was safe. That gave Ajay time to make his escape.

"I only learned what really happened to your parents two years later in 1986. Until then, I believed your parents had been murdered by the rioters. Then, one day, Ajay told me. He wrote it all down and put it in an envelope that he addressed to me. Then he put a gun to his head and blew his brains out."

CHAPTER
Forty

"It happened right here in Vancouver in 1986," Rose said. "We had come here with our son, ostensibly for a visit. In actual fact, however, after everything that had happened in the last two years, I was seriously considering moving here.

"You see our lives changed drastically after Mrs. Gandhi's assassination. Ajay was forced to take early retirement. Suddenly there were no more staff cars, no army of peons, no invitations to embassy parties ... All our friends turned out to be fair weather friends. Ajay often complained bitterly about that. Many times he'd say, 'I did so much for him and now he doesn't even have time to talk to me on the phone.' One time, I responded to that by saying how much I wished that Pritam was still with us. He was the best friend we'd ever had. Ajay just stared at me blankly. Then he turned away and never mentioned his friends again.

"I never got to know what he was really going through inside. Possibly under other circumstances, I would have picked up some clues. But I was much too taken with our son to notice. He was the very center of my existence. After all the trouble I had gone through to get him, I certainly wasn't going to entrust him to the care of ayahs. He was much too precious for that.

"So Ajay was left very much on his own. He had never been a gregarious man in the best of times. Now he retreated even more into himself. He rarely went out. He took to locking himself alone in his study for hours. He found it hard to sleep. Often he was up all night. Once or twice, he even woke up screaming in the middle of the night.

"He became a silent brooding man, increasingly remote even from me. It was only when he was around our son that he showed glimpses of his former self. As the days passed, however, even those moments became fewer and further between. In the end, even the child he had wanted so much wasn't enough to sustain him.

"I attributed the change in Ajay to a number of things; his forced retirement; the fact he had lost all his perks and was now shunned by his friends; the fact he no longer had an office to go to and had to sit about the house the entire day ... I sympathized with him the best I could. However, I had no idea of what was really tearing him up inside. So there was little I could do.

"You see, when Ajay made up his mind to kill your father, he was desperate. He was thinking only of survival. He never stopped for a moment to think he'd have to live with himself once it was done. And even if he had, I doubt if he could have envisioned how hard that would be.

"Would it have been any easier on him if your mother hadn't been in the house? I don't know. Can guilt be sliced like bread into one-half, one-thirds or one-eighths? I don't know that either.

"I do know, however, what really twisted him up inside was what happened to you. I still remember that paragraph, word for word, in the letter he wrote me just before he killed himself. In it he said, 'Because of me this child has lost everything; her home, her family, her friends, her country ... Today she lives in a place that couldn't be much bigger than what was once her pantry, half a world away from where she was born. At a time when she should be looking forward to college, all she has to look forward to is the rent collector. I ask myself: What kind of man could do that to any child, let alone one who was like a daughter to him?'"

"On the second day we were in Vancouver," Rose continued, "Ajay rented a car and drove to Seattle. He told me he wanted to look up an old friend whom he hadn't seen in years; a retired civil servant who was now living with his son and daughter-in-law in Seattle. The son, he told me, was an engineer who worked for Boeing.

"I didn't suspect a thing. Looking back now, I guess I should have. I knew all of Ajay's friends and he had never talked about anyone who lived in Seattle. In fact, I should have questioned the very ease with which I got him to come to Vancouver in the first place. For, by that time, he had stopped leaving the house altogether in Delhi. Yet when I told him that we needed a change and suggested that we go to Vancouver, he agreed immediately. I had expected to argue with him for hours. I guess I was so relieved that I didn't have to argue that I failed to ponder even for a moment on why he accepted so readily.

"My plan was to spend a few weeks in Vancouver. Then I'd talk to Ajay about moving there. Surely, if any place could pull Ajay out of the pit of depression into which he had fallen, it was Vancouver. After all, it was where we met and fell in love. Then, in Vancouver, he'd be far away from Delhi and all its attendant regrets. He could start living again.

"On our second day in Vancouver, when he told me he wanted to go to Seattle, I was actually pleased. I was due to spend the day with some of my old friends from the bar where I had worked before going to India. I knew that wasn't going to be Ajay's cup of tea. So when he said he wanted to go to Seattle, I accepted his reason for going without asking too many questions.

"Now, however, I know that he went to Seattle for the same reason that he came to Vancouver – you.

"He had written you several times over the past two years. You hadn't replied even once. He had tried to get news of how you were doing. But that was difficult. He wasn't in the RAW any longer and he didn't know your uncle or, for that matter, anybody in Seattle. So, finally, he decided he had better go and take a look for himself.

"Maybe he thought he'd feel better if he saw that you were doing okay. He knew the guilt would always stay with him. Nothing in the world could compensate for the loss of your parents. But who knew, maybe if he saw you were doing fine, he'd find a way to live with himself.

"He left early in the morning and drove straight to your uncle's house. There he learned that you had moved. He got the address to your apartment. He went there and found that you were gone. From your landlord, he learned that you worked at a nearby McDonald's. He went there. It was you, all right, standing behind the counter in a McDonald's uniform. He sat down in one corner and watched as you took orders, mopped the floor, cleaned the bathrooms, emptied the dirty trays, took out the trash ... You were much too busy to notice him. You hardly got a moment's breather. By the end of the day, you were so exhausted that you could barely stand. But the worst was yet to come. Just as you were leaving, your manager stopped to have a word with you and gave you the pink slip. She said you were too slow, that the other employees were complaining that they had to cover for you far too much ... You pleaded with her, telling her how much you needed the job. But she refused to budge. Finally, you left with tears in your eyes.

"Ajay followed you as you made your way home. If he had felt bad before, now he felt terrible. If he thought, however, that things couldn't get any worse, he was dead wrong. For you reached home to find an eviction notice stuck on your front door. It said that you were late paying your rent and if you didn't pay within the next three days you would lose your apartment. You went down to talk to your landlord. About ten minutes later, you emerged, looking distraught. You ran all the way to your apartment, banging the door shut behind you.

"Ajay went back to his car to sit motionless behind the wheel. He could very well imagine how you had spent the last two years. The very fact that you should choose to live the kind of life you were leading spoke volumes of the life you must have had in your Uncle's house.

"He hated himself. The guilt he had felt before was now multiplied manifold. From the bottom of his heart, he wished he could go back two years and do everything over.

"As he sat there, a stocky, red-faced man, with greasy graying hair combed back from his forehead, came out on to the street. Ajay recognized him as your landlord. He was the same man who had told him where you worked that morning. He was carrying a bag. Evidently, he was getting ready to go somewhere. He began walking to his car. Before he could get in, however, he was halted by a voice from behind. It was you.

"You walked up to him and said something. Ajay was too far away to hear what it was. When you were finished, however, he saw the man grin wolfishly and slap you on the behind. In spite of yourself, you smiled. The man unlocked his car and opened the door for you, inviting you to get in. You hesitated momentarily. Then you climbed in. Presently, the two of you left.

"Ajay did not follow. He was much too stunned. Not even all the other stuff that had happened that day could have prepared him for what he had just witnessed. For a long time, he simply sat still, gazing unseeingly in front of him.

"Later that night, he drove back to Vancouver. In Vancouver, he sat down at a desk and composed a long letter in which he explained everything. He addressed that letter to me. Then he kissed his son for the last time, put a gun to his head, and blew his brains out."

CHAPTER
Forty-one

Silence filled the room, as both women sat still, immersed in their thoughts. The moments passed slowly. Finally, it was Amrita who broke the silence, speaking in a voice so low it appeared she was talking to herself.

"I was at my wits end," she said. "I needed money. But I had no way of getting any. I had no job or any kind of savings. I couldn't ask my uncle. He had tried his best to talk me out of leaving his house. I didn't think he'd take kindly to me if I went to him barely a month later, asking for money. Furthermore, if I were evicted, I would have no option but to return to his house. Considering how strongly he had argued against my leaving, I felt he'd simply sit back and let me be evicted in order to make me come back. And that was the last thing I wanted. When I left that house, I told myself I wasn't going back, no matter what.

"Somehow I dried my tears and went downstairs and told that man that I'd do what he wanted. It was a Friday. He was going to Portland for the weekend and he had told me if I went along with him he'd forget about the rent. Otherwise, if I didn't have the money by Monday, he'd have me evicted.

"I was able to get into his car. But once I was in that car, I found that I couldn't go through with it. We hadn't even gone a mile when I told him to stop and let me out. Otherwise, I said, I'd start screaming my head off and tell everyone he wanted to rape me. At first he didn't believe me. But when I screamed, he got scared and stopped the car. I jumped out and began to run. I didn't know where I was going. But I just kept running until I was out of breath.

"When I finally got back to my apartment, I threw every piece of clothing I had on into the trash. Then I ran a bath for myself. For hours I lay in the bathtub. I felt so filthy. It was almost as if I had immersed myself in a lake full of muck. My one consolation was that I had gotten out before I drowned.

"The next day I went to my uncle and told him exactly what I needed. He asked me to return to his house. I refused. He wanted to know why I was so set on not coming back. I told him that he, of all people, should know why. That shut him up. He gave me the money

I needed. Little by little I paid him back every penny. He didn't want it back. But I made him take it, anyway.

"I found another job and got out of that apartment as fast as I could. Over the next seven years, I moved frequently. Sometimes I had roommates, other times I lived alone. I was never able to stay at a place long enough for it to be home. More often than not, it was the lack of money that forced me to find a cheaper place to live. At the time, I was trying to make my way through high school, then college. And that took most of my income. It was only after seven years that I found some sort of financial stability. I moved into an apartment in Kent. I've been there the last three years."

She stopped. She was finished. There was a short pause. Then Rose took a deep breath and continued, "After Ajay, there was nothing left for me in India. However, I did have to go back once. We had a house and other assets that had to be taken care of. I went, thinking I'd simply dump everything as fast as I could and come back to Canada. I soon found out that things don't work that way. Disposing off things was much harder than I had imagined. And then, as you can probably see, there were some things I couldn't bear to part with."

She gazed at the picture of Ajay and herself in front of the Taj Mahal. Her eyes grew wistful and a tear glimmered at the edge of one eye. Abruptly, she turned back to Amrita, brushing the tear away.

"If it hadn't been for my son, I don't know how I could have gone on after Ajay," she said. "For after he died, I often wished I too were dead. I even thought of killing myself. But even in my darkest moments, my son was always there at the back of my mind. I knew, for his sake, I had to live.

"And slowly, I began to live again. I went back to the university and completed the masters I had interrupted to get married. Then I got a job, teaching at a girls' school. I chose a teaching job so that I could have the afternoons with my son. Gradually, I started building a life for both of us. The money wasn't much, but at least it was steady. As the years passed and I moved up, it got better. My real joy, however, was my son. Watching him grow up has been the best part of my life. This year he turned thirteen. He is everything I could have ever wanted. His father would have been proud of him."

A smile lit up her face, as she paused momentarily, thinking of her son. Then she said, "At the end of the last school year, the Board of Governors of my school informed me that I was to be the new headmistress once our present headmistress retires at the end of this year. That put to rest any worries I might have had for the future. On a headmistress' salary, I was sure I'd manage just fine, while sending my son to a good college. For the first time in years, I felt secure.

"And then I met Gurbachan Singh."

CHAPTER
Forty-two

"It was my husband's death anniversary," Rose said. "On that day, every year, I visit a Hindu temple and a Sikh gurudwara. Ajay was a traditional Punjabi, who didn't distinguish between Hindus and Sikhs. He would have wanted the anniversary of his death observed in both places of worship.

"This year I visited a new gurudwara. I had recently moved and the gurudwara I had frequented for the last twelve years was too far away. So I went to another one which was much closer.

"I said my prayers and made my offering. Then I came out and was untying the scarf I had used to cover my head when an old Sikh man approached me with folded hands and said, namaste, memsahib.

"He was Gurbachan Singh. He had met me in Delhi at the home of the Director General of Supplies and Disposals. My husband and I were often invited to parties there and Gurbachan Singh was one of the servers.

"He looked terrible. His kurta was stained; apparently, it hadn't been washed for days. The rubber slippers he had on were crumbling. And he was altogether much too thin.

"We talked for a few minutes. It was a difficult conversation. I had practically forgotten the Hindi and Punjabi I had picked up in Delhi. And he didn't speak English too well. However, somehow we were able to communicate. He asked about Ajay. I told him that Ajay had died in an accident. Then I asked him what he was doing in Vancouver. He said he was living with his nephew who had an Indian restaurant in the West End. Just from looking at him, I could visualize the kind of life he must be leading. While shopping for Indian groceries, I would often pick up a copy of one of the local Indian newspapers. In them, I'd invariably find a story dealing with the plight of aging relatives that had come over to Canada. Gurbachan Singh, from all appearances, embodied everything that I had read.

"I gave him some money. He didn't want to take it. But I pushed it into his hands, nevertheless. I also gave him my address and phone number and told him to get in touch with me if he ever needed anything. Then I said good-bye.

"I didn't hear from him for three months. Then one day I got a phone call. He wanted to see me immediately. He said it was very important. He sounded disturbed. I told him I'd meet him that evening.

"We met at an Indian restaurant in Surrey. There he told me that he had seen you at a wedding three weeks ago. Ever since then, he had been wrestling with himself. Thirteen years ago, upon learning of your father's death, he had figured out that your father had actually been murdered. How? Well, as he said, he figured he'd be having coffee with him at that moment if he had refused to play ball with Ajay. For thirteen years, he had kept his mouth shut. Now he couldn't stay quiet any longer.

"He said he had done a lot of soul searching in the last three weeks. And he had come to the conclusion the best thing for him to do was to make a clean breast of everything. He had nothing to look forward to in life. All he could do now was atone for his sins so that he could die in peace. I had always been good to him. So he felt it was his duty to tell me before he acted.

"Needless to say, I was taken aback. It took me some time to recover. When I did, I begged him to reconsider. I told him my husband had paid dearly for what he did; he was dead by his own hand. All I had left was a son who would be devastated if he learned his father was a murderer. Why, I had never even told my son that his father had killed himself. I had simply said that he had died in an accident. Gurbachan Singh was welcome to take anything I had. But please, if he told you or anyone about Ajay, he could destroy the life I had built for myself and my son.

"I argued with him for hours. I beseeched him. I even attempted to bribe him. Again and again, I brought up the impact such revelations could have on my son ... He appeared to waver slightly. But not enough. When the restaurant closed for the night and it was time for us to leave, he was still determined to go ahead.

"I went back home with my mind in turmoil. There my son was waiting for me, even though it was well past his bedtime. He wanted to show me something he had made in his art class.

It turned out to be a painting of his father that he had done from one of his old photographs.

"Tears filled my eyes. My son, not able to figure out why I was crying, asked me if he had done something wrong. Unable to speak, I simply shook my head and hugged him close.

"A little later, I dried my eyes and put him to bed. As I was saying good night, he asked if he could get the painting of his father framed and hang it up in his room. Once again, a lump entered my throat. I said, of course he could. He was happy. He kissed me good night and went to sleep.

"I stayed in his room a little longer, just watching him lying there. He had been only two at the time of his father's death. Yet he felt such a deep affection for him. What if he learned his father was a murderer ...

"O, if only Gurbachan Singh would somehow go away, disappear from the face of the earth ... People disappeared all the time. They got run over by cars. They had heart attacks. They even killed themselves ... Why, just recently, I had read in a local Indian newspaper about an elderly man in Toronto who had swallowed a cyanide pill, because he was fed up of being neglected by his children. From what I had seen, Gurbachan Singh's life wasn't that different from that man's life. So if he killed himself, I doubted if it would come as too much of a surprise to anyone.

"I guess that was the beginning. Sometime during that night, I began more than merely wish for him to disappear; I began planning his disappearance.

"Just six months ago, when our dog became terminally ill, I had procured some cyanide pills from a friend who was a chemist. I still had a few left. They were more than enough to do the job. I figured, if I took the pills with me and went to Gurbachan Singh's house sometime after nine the next morning, there was a good chance that I would find him on his own. Gurbachan Singh had told me his nephew and his nephew's wife left for work at nine and the kids were at school by eight. So he was alone in the house from nine until the kids returned from school in the afternoon. That would give me plenty of time to get the job done.

"I wrote the suicide note in the morning. In it, I cited neglect and loneliness as the chief reasons for the suicide. I put it in my handbag with the cyanide. Gurbachan Singh lived in an Indian neighborhood. So I put on a salwar kameez, with a dupatta to cover my hair. I also placed a bindi on my forehead and put on dark glasses to hide my eyes.

"Then I went over to his house. There everything went according to plan. I rang the doorbell and Gurbachan Singh let me in. Nobody saw me go into the house, or for that matter, come out. Gurbachan Singh was too weak to put up any kind of struggle. And when everyone accepted that his death was a suicide, I thought I was safe. What I didn't know was that Gurbachan Singh had already written to you."

CHAPTER
Forty-three

"You thought of everything," Amrita said. "And then you wrote the suicide note in English."

Rose shook her head with a wry smile. "And I thought I'd done it like a real pro," she said.

There was a short pause. Then Rose said, "Now you know everything. So what are you going to do?"

Amrita didn't answer.

"After Gurbachan Singh you have nothing that ties Ajay to the murder of your parents in any way," Rose said. "And after thirteen years you won't find anything. And as for me – nobody saw me go in and out of the house, nobody saw me kill Gurbachan Singh, I even changed my handwriting when I wrote the note ... You'll be hardpressed to prove anything against me.

"There is really nothing you can do, Amrita, nothing."

"Why do I have to do anything?" Amrita demanded. "Your husband murdered my parents and look what happened to him. In the end even the son he wanted to protect couldn't save him. I didn't have to do anything. So why should I have to do anything to you?"

She stared at Rose, challenging her to refute what she had just said. Rose stared back. Then Rose's face fell. Her shoulders sagged. She looked sad, tired, shrunken ...

Amrita rose and walked out of the house without a backward glance.

EPILOGUE

When she came out of Rose's house, she found Deepak and Jaswant standing outside in the rain. They were drenched to the skin. Deepak surprised her by throwing his arms around her and hugging her close. When he finally released her, he appeared just as taken aback as she was with what he had just done. Jaswant told her that they had been getting more and more concerned about her with each passing minute. Another five minutes and they would have come in.

They all got into the car and drove to an all-night diner. After

Deepak and Jaswant had dried themselves in the bathroom, Amrita related what had happened at Rose's house. The two men listened, as they ate. When she was finished, there was silence. Then Jaswant said that he didn't know about the two of them, but he was bushed and wanted to go to bed. He suggested they clear the bill and get back to the motel. Amrita concurred. She was spent as well.

The next morning, when she came down to the motel lobby for breakfast, she found Deepak waiting for her. Jaswant, he said, was sleeping in. Amrita glanced in the direction of the breakfast trays to find them empty.

"Looks like we are late," she said.

"Yes, it certainly does."

"You want to go somewhere else?"

"Okay."

"There is a Starbucks across the street."

"I've never had breakfast in one before."

"Come on, it'll be fine."

They went to the Starbucks. There he asked her what he should eat. He said he didn't want anything sweet. Instead, he preferred something salty, a little spicy, perhaps. After some thought, she suggested a cheese twist. When the barista served it up, he examined it with interest.

"This reminds me of a cat's leg," he said.

"What?" she said.

"A cat's leg. Just look at the way the bread is shaped."

"Oh."

He took a bite and nodded approvingly. After sipping his tea, however, he grimaced.

"In the West they make their tea too light and their coffee too strong," he said.

He put his cup down and leaned back in his chair, gazing at the woman seated across the table from him. For the first time, he noticed two tiny lines below her eyes and the beginning of a wrinkle at the edge of her eyebrows. Somehow it all seemed to make her even more attractive – the beautiful woman rather than the cute girl.

Last night, he had barely been able to contain himself when she had been alone with Rose. Until she came back, nothing else had mattered except her safe return. Not his career, not Mrs. Gandhi's murder ... When she finally did come back, he had been so overcome with relief that he had stepped completely out of character and embraced her. The whole of last night, he had lain awake, recalling that moment, which, more than anything, showed him how much he had come to care for her in the brief time they had known each other.

Now he wished for nothing more than to share that revelation with her. But he found himself hesitating. He felt stiff, awkward. Even words, that usually obeyed his call, appeared intent on failing him.

In the end, it was she who broke the silence by asking, "What will you do now?"

"I don't know," he said.

"Well, there are still some unanswered questions about Mrs. Gandhi."

"Yes, I guess there are."

"And there should be a story in the fact that people in intelligence had advance warning of the fatal attempt on Mrs. Gandhi's life and did nothing about it."

"Yes, I guess there should be."

They were both quiet. Then, after a short pause, Deepak asked, "What about you?"

"Me?"

"Yes, what will you do?"

"Well, ever since I was a girl I have wanted to be a doctor. Next year I should have enough money for medical school. I guess that's where I'll go."

"And then?"

"*Then*?"

"After medical school. What will you do then?"

She was silent. For so long she had focused on simply getting to medical school, without once stopping to think what she'd do afterwards.

"I don't know," she said. "When I was a girl I had all sorts of plans about going to Africa and helping sick people like Albert Schweitzer. But now ..."

She shrugged her shoulders. For a moment, they sat in silence. Then Deepak said, "You know after I learned that Gurbachan Singh had written to you, I tried to find out stuff about you. When I found out where you worked, I called the place. I wanted to know what time you got off so that I could talk to you. The guy who picked up the phone in the clinic placed my accent immediately. It was the doctor himself. It was lunch break, he said, and you were out to lunch like everyone else. Then he told me what I wanted to know. However, just as I was ringing off, he asked me a strange question. He asked if I was the guy from India to whom you had been promised in marriage."

He took a deep breath.

"Is there such a man in India?" he asked.

Amrita hesitated, but only for an instant.

"No," she said, smiling.